A LITTLE MORE THAN KIN

Also by Rebecca Kavaler

THE FURTHER ADVENTURES OF BRUNHILD
TIGERS IN THE WOOD
DOUBTING CASTLE

A LITTLE MORE THAN KIN

A Collection of Short Stories

REBECCA **K**AVALER

HAMILTON STONE EDITIONS
Maplewood, N.J.

Copyright 2001 Rebecca Kavaler

LIBRARY OF CONGRESS CATALOGING-IN-PUBLICATION DATA
Kavaler, Rebecca.
    A little more than kin : a collection of stories / by Rebecca Kavaler.
        p. cm.
    Contents: Give brother my best — Sisters — Mother — Inheritance — Pets — Servants —
Mysteries — Pigeons.
    ISBN 0-9654043-8-2 (pbk.)
    1. Domestic fiction, American. 2. United States—Social life and customs—20th century—
Fiction. I. Title.
PS3561.A868 L58 2001
813'.54—dc21   2001024532

Book Design by Cheryl L. Cipriani/Brooklyn Bauhaus

These stories originally appeared in the following publications:

"Give Brother My best," *Carolina Quarterly*
"Sister," *American Short Fiction*
"Mother," *Other Voices*
"The Inheritance," *Shenandoah*
"Mysteries," *Confrontation*
"Pigeons," *Other Voices*

And less than kind...

HAMLET, ACT 1, SCENE 2

CONTENTS

GIVE BROTHER
MY BEST

I HATE FAMILY AFFAIRS. I HAVE COME BACK FROM THIS last one irritable, depressed. The wedding of a daughter of a cousin of my husband's mother—I had to laugh. You call that a family, I asked my husband on the way back, this monstrous aggregate, inflated to gargantuan size with uncles, aunts, cousins, in-laws, whose vociferous greetings will be followed by complete silence until the next occasion. An occasional family. No wedding, anniversary, birth, funeral occurs but kinship is reasserted like a ritual oath. They convoke like the annual congress of a professional society, whose members have no personal ties, nothing in common beyond the shop talk of their kinsman trade.

Even to his brother and sister my husband is polite, presents what I recognize as his company face, as if they had never lived together in one house where doors slammed with hate, wills clashed in hot kitchens, cold beds were for plotting, sides were taken at the dining table, and jokes exploded like fireworks, shattering faces with laughter.

We were a *real* family—Brother and Sister, Mama and Daddy—marked like cards in an Old Maid deck, answering to no other name. Flesh and blood. Flesh and blood. That was Mama's call to arms. That was the family. Yet it was more than that: it was her hard stony virgin plot carved out of the wilderness of the world. She had seeded it, weeded it, nourished it, guarded it; within its confines her flesh and blood would grow, flourish, multiply—who knows what homey touch of megalomania distinguished her dreams? Meanwhile, to Brother and me, the thought of ever living beyond that tightly defined territory was as fantastic as the exploration of outer space.

Before the front door of our house we shed neighbors and school friends as meticulously as if we were Japanese removing shoes soiled with the outdoors. When guests did penetrate into the living room, the barricades were not dismantled, merely drawn back a few yards to the corridor of bedroom doors, firmly closed. No one ever dropped in. The rare visitors were heralded far in advance, and then Mama's hospitality was magnificent. Cake was baked, ice cream cranked in the freezer on the back porch, the good china and crystal brought down from the top of the kitchen cupboard to gleam more conspicuously on open shelves. Curtains were washed and ironed, and the faded cretonne slipcovers removed from the sofa to display the maroon plush upholstery, bought in the prosperous twenties but now afflicted with bald patches of worn nap like an elegant disease of the rich. So two chivalric armies might meet on a field of gold, the glitter of raiment and trappings, the mouthing of politenesses, the formal alignment of forces (Mama always in a straight-back chair moved in from the dining room, facing her guests, never sitting along side of them)—all this was but the daily warfare continued in another mode.

The war was all in Mama's mind, but to us she projected her hallucinations with greater force than reality could muster. She was a Northerner buried in the deep South, a Lutheran awash in Baptist waters, a stranger with no blood kin within a thousand miles. Daddy, if allowed, would have defected to the enemy long ago—poor Daddy, with his cocker spaniel soul—but Mama played grim watchdog over us all.

Even Brother and I, hating each other as only close kin do, felt joined together in our differences from all others. Come in and see my dolls, a school friend would say, swinging on her screen door until someone inside ordered her to close it to keep the flies out. Hesitantly I would enter—knowing no such invitation could come from me—walk through the dark front hall on timid tiptoe, like a wild animal scenting some trap, not touching anything, not even the handle of a door, letting it be opened for me, making my friend walk through first, and, again like an animal, most terrified because the very smell of her house was different from the smell of ours.

To this day I don't know what was different about the smell. Our floors were scrubbed with the same harsh yellow Octagon soap, our clothes boiled in the same black pots over the same wood fires, and for the most part we ate the same food. Mama's cooking had slid imperceptibly into the Southern idiom of deep-fat frying, cream sauces, hot biscuits and cornbread. Perhaps twice a year, as if militantly reaffirming her Pennsylvania origins, she made her own scrapple and baked a shoofly pie, which, without liking overmuch, we accepted on the table solemnly, like the bitter herbs of a Jewish seder.

The frequent moves from one neighborhood to another followed the exigencies of Daddy's disastrous business career. With each bankruptcy came ignominious removal: Mama more proud, we more shy, the family more close-knit. Only Daddy remained incorrigible, both in winning friends and losing money—linked in Mama's mind as cause and effect, further acidulating her misanthropy.

I remember her railing: "Out to lunch, out to lunch— you were out to lunch four hours—four hours by the clock—from the time I first phoned until you finally answered. Customers could be beating on the door and where are you? Out to lunch!" Mama's virulence lent itself at times to such extravagance. None of us, not even she, could really imagine customers beating on the door. And she knew he was not eating lunch, but out somewhere with the "boys," playing cards, fishing, hunting or perhaps just leaning over a Coke machine swapping jokes. It was, after all, the Great Depression, and lunch or no lunch, his little businesses were no doubt doomed to failure—the gas station, the radio repair shop, the ice cream parlor, the food brokerage where for several months he hovered in some nebulous purgatory between wholesale and retail and ended up with twenty cases of canned goods on which we lived for several weeks.

Nevertheless, this "out to lunch" sign inevitably became a neighborhood joke. It was one of those signs with a painted clock face and two cardboard hands to position at the hour of intended return. When he left at noon, he would set the hands at one, but the slightest jar of the door would cause them to collapse on six-thirty. If the hands did not fall of their own accord, some prankster would see to it.

Bankruptcy always proved Mama's point, and in the bustle of moving she would bludgeon Daddy with cheerfulness: "At least there's no place to go now but up." When we moved to Beecham Street, however, she said nothing at all.

Beecham Street climbed straight up a hill and there on the crown was the Federal Penitentiary. Al Capone was housed there. As I remember it, this was our claim to fame, *Gone with the Wind* not yet having been written. The hill had been bare when the prison was built but now its sides were scored with narrow streets studded with boxlike frame bungalows, rectangular, monotonous, cheap. Always before, wherever we lived, no matter how old and decrepit and rambling the structure—even if a flat of rooms over a store—we could find just down the block, sometimes next door, a fine house, at least some substantial ones. Street addresses gave nothing away: our income, our social position were shaded under a leafy ambiguity. But Beecham

Street was the first of those new developments—presaging the low-income housing projects yet to come—of houses built at the same time by the same contractor to the same plan for the same people. Poor people. A little mill town without a mill. Although, now that I think of it, the Pen could have passed for one. Many old factories had the same fierce brick castellated air.

No need here for shrieking chalk reminders of the wages of sin or the imminent approach of the kingdom of heaven. At night the searchlights playing over the prison yard rhythmically swooped across bedroom windows and in the dark the sleepers shuddered as if diddled by the finger of God. No longer was "the Boogie-man will get you if you don't watch out" childhood's cautionary refrain. Instead, "you'll wind up in the Pen some day," we were promised. The Boogie-man we could outgrow but the Pen was always there and we didn't have far to go. Like the fine steady settling of soot from the prison chimneys, rectitude rained on us.

Mama settled herself in this new house, shivering like the emperor who for the first time felt the nakedness of his new clothes. It was then I am sure she gave up on Daddy. It was then she must have turned to Brother as the great white hope of the family.

Remembering Brother as he was then, I can see why. That was the summer of—'36, '37?—somewhere around then. He was to enter high school in the fall with straight A's behind him. I suppose that even as a child he was unusually attractive—what big eyes you have, people were always telling him (my eyes were just as big but no one ever said so). And that summer something happened to him that even I could see—it was like the brightness of a star exploding into the blinding blaze of a supernova, so that Mama's eyes, when she looked at him, watered like the eyes of someone who has stared too long at the sun. His voice had changed without cracking, his good looks hung on the edge of manliness without once stumbling into pimples and gawkiness. Girls were crazy about him, older girls—he was tall for his age—but it was more than that. Even grown-ups clustered around him like flies after honey. Mama was proud of his good manners. He spoke up with assurance, never squirmed or fidgeted, and always remembered to say sir or ma'am. Only Daddy found something to be displeased about, but just what he couldn't put his finger on. Smart-alecky, was the term he finally settled for.

"Smart-alecky," he complained to Mama, "did you hear him with Ben Chalmers? A man like that." That was right after the junior high graduation, when Mr. Chalmers had made a speech and given out prizes, two of them to Brother. Mr. Chalmers was something big in the Chamber of Commerce and also something big in a charitable organization that devoted its good works to fatherless boys. After the exercises, he took Brother aside to congratulate him, returned him to Mama and Daddy with words of warm praise. He was a big moon-faced man, with a button nose and the rimless glasses that were considered most becoming in those days—the first man I had smelled, not counting sweat. It must have been a scented shaving lotion. That and the French cuffs on his shirt sleeves placed him in a class far above us.

"You don't know what you're talking about," Mama refuted Daddy bluntly, for Mr. Chalmers had offered Brother a part-time summer job, which showed what a good impression Brother had made. And it was she who insisted that Brother accept, called him lazy—"just like your father"—when he hesitated.

"I know you," she scolded fondly, "you want to spend all summer in the swimming pool like last year, but you're old enough now, Brother, to begin thinking about your future. It's good Christian work, too, helping Mr. Chalmes on outings for those poor little boys, it'll do you no harm to learn that there are others less fortunate than you."

The only time I remember Mama ever admitting that. Her platform for life called for never looking down, only up. It was Daddy who pointed out the cripples and told us, with the complacent cheerfulness of a man who has left his children well provided for, to thank God we had two arms and two legs. Mama, on the other hand, directed our Sunday afternoon rides—the current price wars among the gas stations made this the cheapest entertainment—to the most exclusive residential areas of the city where fabulous estates could be glimpsed behind fortress-like walls. She had a cheerfulness of her own in pointing out to us, whenever a rise in the ground or a turn in the road permitted, a spot of Gothic tower or a ripple of red Spanish tile, as if all this grandeur was our inheritance from *her*, once a few legal formalities were gone through.

Brother at least seemed to get the message, and that summer began his ascent. Effortlessly. That was the crux of the matter—. without any effort at all. What Mama's imagination had seen as a great sword-clashing battle, calling for rigorous training, adventurous daring, persistent attack—for which she had forged the virtue of the family's ways, the purity of its vision, the strength of its cohesion— Brother promised to achieve with just his blue eyes. And his blond hair combed into a high wave. As effortlessly as his sun-browned arms swooped up and cut down to cleave the water.

Mr. Chalmers had taken him under his wing and his patronage promised more for the future than a part-time summer job. Mama and Daddy whispered together about college scholarships or even a West Point appointment for which Mr. Chalmers had the necessary congressman in his pocket. Daddy was particularly pleased with that congressman. He mentioned him often, hands in his own pocket, jingling coins in vicarious affluence. The afternoon I caught Brother at a city swimming pool when he was supposed to be on the job—and of course told on him—Mama had a fit. Didn't Brother realize the importance of making good on this summer job? Didn't he know what depended on it? What, she demanded of him, would Mr. Chalmers think if he played hookey like that?

He's really caught it this time, I thought with some satisfaction, but Brother just slapped his wet towel and suit over the back porch railing, poured a cold drink from the ice box, combed his still-damp hair in the hall mirror— Mama ever on his heels eloquent with prophecies of disaster—picked up the tightly rolled afternoon paper on the front porch and began to read the funnies. Desperate, she tore it out of his hands and swatted him with it. He looked at her with the same sulky air of forbearance he assumed when she nagged him about homework or criticized his friends.

"Did you at least call the man and tell him you were sick?" she pleaded.

"Yes," Brother said, eyeing the funnies, "I called him."

Mama sighed in defeat and gave him back the paper. "Well, I hope nobody else saw you at the pool. These things get around, you know."

Brother snickered, already deep in the funnies. But because she continued to stand over him in a gloom of worry, he threw her a reassurance. "You're getting upset over nothing, Mama, it's not that kind of a job. I can do pretty much what I please, that's the way Mr. Chalmers wants it."

Mama didn't believe it. To her there was only one kind of a job: you worked hard, you applied yourself, you made good. But she had to admit that Brother's way seemed the way Mr. Chalmers wanted it. Brother not only kept the job but was granted guest privileges at Mr. Chalmers' country club, where he could practice swimming in an Olympic-sized pool and mingle with the wealthy on terms that to us at home, overhearing telephone calls, were frighteningly chummy.

Whatever kind of a job it was, Brother continued to have plenty of time for swimming. At the midsummer swim meet, he turned out to be the star. That boy should be trained for the Olympics, was what Daddy overheard.

Mama and I missed that—at the last moment I had vomited, been put to bed, and Daddy had driven off alone with Brother. It must have been a great night—the outdoor pool in Grant Park especially lit up, temporary bleachers for the city notables, a big shirt-sleeved crowd sucked to the water's edge by the black-velvet summer heat. As a swimmer Brother was good, but it was on the high dive that he leaped into greatness. I know very well how he walked out on the board, gave a few little test springs, stood there with his arms upraised, motionless, the muscles of his stomach taut, manufacturing drama in the stillness and the silence, as if a drum were rolling. Poor Mama, she had to wait until they got back to hear all about it, and I woke up too, fully recovered, to listen to Daddy's midnight account of glory.

For me, that became the great occasion—being up in the middle of the night with darkened houses all around us, but our light still burning—the neighbors blotted out by sleep and we alone, a small tight conclave of life huddled together around the kitchen table under the protecting circle of the harsh overhead light. This was the family, I saw it so for the first time although I know now this is the way Mama always saw it. I could even see the kinship of our faces, faces that before had been unique. Mine would grow long and elastic, drooping unaware into ludicrous moues like Daddy's while Brother shared the broad-browed, blunt-nosed handsomeness of Mama's. Only his had a fleshiness, packed firmly (for he was so young) around his wide nostrils, rounding his cheeks, filling out his lips, that I doubt hers had ever known. Certainly as I remember hers, it had squared off against the world into granite hardness, only her eyes—hazel, not blue—small, retiring under the bony ridge, still soft and uncongealed.

"He came over and introduced himself—he's a friend of Ben Chalmers—it seems Ben's been bragging about you, Brother—and said that boy of yours sure can dive and I said, well, he's not bad for his age, and he said not bad? why that boy'll be state champion before he graduates, you mark my words, he ought to start training right now for the Olympics—that's what he said, Brother—and then he just up and asked me to come on out to his plant and pick me a bushel of peaches before they're all gone—free, I made sure of that, Mama—and bring your boy too, he said, he can have all he can eat."

Mr. Haskell. I remember his name, but not much else about him. Just another notch on Brother's gun belt, I thought that night. A strange lady stops me on the street. I smirk, at last I am noticed, admired. But she asks, is that your brother, child? I had my own fantasies: Shirley Temple surrounded by the Damon Runyon crowd, Merrylips among the Cavaliers. Only to Brother it happened in real life, like this—the invitation to all the peaches he could eat.

Daddy had fantasies of his own, Brother's success having gone to his head. "Your Mr. Chalmers had better watch out," he said, nudging Brother, "I think Mr. Haskell aims to steal you away from him. Asked me if you needed a part-time job. Says he's got one open in his town office that pays real good. You find out how much, Brother, then we'll see." His laugh embraced and swallowed up Brother. "We'll see, yessir, we'll see," he repeated, as if it were the punch line of a joke.

We drove out the next day in spite of Mama's warning. "I hope you know what you're doing. Chances are he won't know you from Adam, so you'd better be ready to pay for them."

The peaches I remember. The smell of them bruised, in bushel baskets piled high outside the corrugated tin of the packing plant. The white heat of mid-afternoon in a hot July. Flies thick as dust flurries, carousing in the odoriferous air. Peaches purpled, sunken-cheeked, skinned raw in spots, stinking sweet. I can feel my mouth pucker over the fuzz of the peel before my teeth bite through into the juicy flesh.

Only Daddy and Brother went into the shed. I unstuck my sweaty behind from the seat to follow, but Mama grabbed hold of my skirt and pulled me back. Miss Tagalong, she called me on such occasions. "You just climb back in the car, Miss Tagalong. That's no place for a child." Or for a girl. If it wasn't one, it was the other—life was one enormous plot to get me out of the way. I suppose I howled, because Mama turned around in her seat and swung her purse at me. It missed by a mile. It always did the first time, just as the second time it would land hard, smack against the cheek. Her purse was of black leather, supple and worn, fat sides bulging, and with it Mama swung all the weight and authority of the household. It held her department store bills, with itemized sales slips. It held letters from her Pennsylvania relatives and empty envelopes she was saving for the return address. It held her three bankbooks—she never trusted any one bank again, not after they had closed down on her in '33, but parceled out her small savings among several. It held shopping lists and receipts for gas and light and water. It was her safe, her office file, her household ledger. It was as sanctified a symbol of power as the Roman lictor's bundle of rods with the embedded axe, and after it swished once threateningly over my head, I sprawled submissive for the moment in the back seat.

Someone appeared at the entrance of the shed, a tall man in a wilted seersucker suit. Mr. Haskell? Daddy took off his panama and wiped the top of his head apologetically, like a man asking for directions. The man laughed and shook Daddy's hand, and then put his hand on Brother's head, rubbing it playfully. They went inside, into the cool-seeming darkness, with the man's arm thrown over Daddy's shoulders. Just before he vanished, I saw Brother reaching into his hip pocket for his comb.

"Hot as an oven," Mama complained, "they'd better not be long."

Everything is still in that white heat. The noise from the packing plant reaches us as a soft soporific hum. The faintest threads of white cloud in the sky, as if there the faded blue canvas was wearing thin. In the tall sedge grass, not one stalk stirring. The busyness of insects mounts in a buzz, drone, chirrup, crackle. Mama's head nods, her eyes close. I wait for the definitive snore.

It came at last, a beautiful musical sound, like the whistle of a peanut vender's machine. And I was out the window, scuffing my bare feet in the thick dust.

The walls of the shed were fringed with weeds, bone-dry, heat-yellowed, which cracked loudly as I sidled through them. At first I peered cautiously through the open door, lest Daddy see me and send me back, and then sneaked through to glue my backbone to the inside wall, the way we practiced good posture in p.t. class. It made me feel flatter, more nearly invisible. In the center of the shed, throughout its length, women were paddling their arms in a trough of peaches, a wrist flicking here and there, removing a discard, sizing, grading, intent as miners panning gold. Around them moved bare-torsoed men, shouldering the baskets in and out, loading them on flat trolleys. No seersucker suit to be seen anywhere. I finally located Daddy over by a Coke machine at the far end of the shed, drinking and talking and laughing with two men.—foremen, no doubt, for they wore shirts. He had his jacket folded over his arm and he was leaning against the machine with his thumb hooked over his belt, and I could tell he wasn't going any place soon. He always looked different to me when I saw him like that, away from us, among strangers.

For one thing, he didn't look at all like the "married man with two children to feed," which was Mama's reiterated definition of him. There he slouched, long-limbed and thin and as gawky with his height as if he had just shot up over the summer and wasn't used to it yet, his tight round pot-belly no more than a sofa pillow tucked in a boy's shirt. And when he had finished his joke and one of the other men had started on his, I saw how he listened, his long face poised on the starting-line of laughter, his two big front teeth, with the child-like gap between them, biting down over his bottom lip in delight. Whereas at home, playing father of two children with insatiable appetites, he rounded his shoulders and pulled down the lines of his face, and didn't say much, and when he looked at us, his glance skittered nervously away, as if—eye to eye—we might catch on he was just pretending to great worries, to please Mama.

Of course it was that utter inability to appreciate disaster that drove Mama wild, but to me, a child, to whom only fun and play were real too, he seemed wholly wonderful then. That afternoon in the packing shed I hated and envied Brother as never before, seeing that Daddy could look like that when they went off together but never at home with me.

I had not noticed until then that Brother wasn't there. I looked all over but he wasn't in the shed at all. Nor, I remembered, was the seersucker suit. One of the workmen approached the Coke machine, hiking up his khaki pants in shy subservience before he spoke to the shirted men, much as in another age he would have tugged at a forelock and bent a knee. One of them looked out over the heads of the workers and called "Mr. Haskell!" You could tell that was the name of the boss; all the noise stopped, the rattle of trolleys ceased, people stood still and looked up and around and at each other. There was no answer. With all those eyes searching him out, I could not hope to stand there unseen. I inched my way back to the door and out into the blinding brightness.

Wherever Brother was, he was with Mr. Haskell. I pictured him gorging on peaches, all he could eat. I would have all I could eat too when Daddy finally carted the bushel basket to the car, but it wasn't the same. I wanted to be hand-fed, like Brother, by someone who smiled down on me the way the man in the seersucker suit had smiled down on him, a two-way smile that asked as much as it

gave. Stubborn on the scent, I skirted the side of the building where the trucks were drawn up and rounded it to the
back. There was nothing there but broken crates and baskets, some enormous garbage cans, and the kind of little
junk piles of rubber tires, empty oil cans, rusty bits of
machinery that every plant drops like excrement at its rear.
Beyond the wide field of sedge grass, matted down by the
crisscrossing of innumerable tracks, the orchard took over,
precisely marching to the horizon. I almost missed them.
A few more steps and they would have seen me before I
saw them, standing in the shade of the single stray peach
tree that grew almost next to the shed, as if one long summer ago somebody had happened to spit out a seed there.

I kept back behind the garbage cans, at a loss for my
next move. They were talking but I couldn't hear what they
said. Mr. Haskell had his hand on Brother's shoulder. With
a playfulness that somehow offended me to see in a grown-
up man, he reached inside Brother's shirt and tickled his
back, offending Brother too apparently, for he squirmed
away and started back to the shed. I crouched lower and
no longer peered around the can but I could hear them
now. I heard Mr. Haskell's voice, deep, unctuous ,bent on
pleasing, and everything he said began with a chuckle and
ended with a laugh, like quotation marks attributing the
words in between to someone else. "I'll fix it up with your
daddy about the game next Saturday—the way I hear it
from Ben, you're quite a baseball fan." And I heard Brother
reply, politely enough to make Mama proud, "Well sir, if
you want to know the truth, I can take it or leave it—baseball, I mean—but I'll take it, so long as I get the money

first." Mr. Haskell chuckled deeper, "Don't you trust me, son?" he asked and laughed louder and Brother said, "Oh yes sir, it would sort of spoil things if I couldn't, sir." Even I could hear the insolence seeping through that last belated title of respect but Mr. Haskell just chuckled and laughed again but with nothing in between this time.

They re-entered the shed and I made a dash for the car, my only concern at the moment to be safely sprawled on the back seat when Mama woke up. Only with her head again lolling heavily in front of me, did I consider the significance of what I had heard. That Mr. Haskell should not only take Brother to a ball game but pay for the privilege. Farewell to Shirley Temple and goodbye Merrylips—inept fantasies dissolved once and for all in the acid bath of reality, that clear view snatched from behind a garbage can, of the supreme potency of Brother's charms.

They came back soon with the bushel of peaches, and Mama woke up and examined the basket critically. "How much did you pay for them?" she asked suspiciously when she couldn't find any rotten ones even beneath the top layer.

"They were free, I tell you," Daddy said, wearing again his worried "family-man" face. "Brother made a hit with Mr. Haskell all right. He's taking him to the ball game Saturday," he added quickly, probably to soften her up, and she was pleased and good-humored all the way home.

It was months later—no longer the baseball but the football season—before I found out no one else knew about the money. By then it had become a ritual on Sunday morning for Brother to turn over to Mama his weekly part-time earnings. Before she held out her hands, she wiped them on her apron and he prolonged the show by carefully unrolling and smoothing out the crumpled wadded-up bills and stacking the coins in neat piles. And she counted it out all over again, impressing us with the magnificent total—ten, sometimes fifteen dollars—her fingers spinning the coins from the table into her palm with a storekeeper's computer speed. Although the summer job was over, he seemed to be making just as much from the caddying he did at the country club. Some of the loose change was always returned to him for pocket-money—more than Daddy thought good for him I have no doubt for there was always something sly about the way Mama folded up Brother's fingers around the coins, sealing his fist with a fond tap.

His birthday fell on a Sunday that year and on that occasion Mama enclosed a green bill in his hand. Even Brother was amazed when he saw that it was a five, not a single. The next day he spent it all on a wallet, a genuine leather one; more than that, a leather we had never seen before—tough as pigskin but the grain pocked with little puckered circles like embroidered eyelets. Ostrich, he told us, and we were certainly awed. Five dollars for a wallet—five dollars! That was enough for a week's groceries if you were careful to buy the specials. Mama had to fight back her tears but Daddy laughed so loud in a woman it would have sounded hysterical. It became one of his pet stories about Brother, that fine ostrich wallet: "All his money for a wallet, and nothing left to put in it!"

It was the wallet that gave him away. Mama had come into the bathroom to clean up after Brother's bath—she always complained about having to do that, but still she did it. There, with his dirty sneakers, wet towel, underwear, she had found the ostrich wallet. She called him, all set to hand it over after the usual lecture about his untidiness and carelessness—"money doesn't grow on trees, you know"— when she noticed how thick the wad of green was. He grabbed for it but she blocked him with that hard square shoulder of hers and counted forty-seven dollars.

She couldn't make a sound. It was Brother's yell that brought Daddy and me running. When Daddy saw the money, his face reddened in blotches as if he had just been slapped and he croaked, "Even I don't carry around that kind of money."

Of course they were sure he had stolen it. Daddy kept threatening to call the police, but neither Mama nor Brother paid any attention to him. They kept eyeing each other like two crouching wrestlers waiting to get a stranglehold. Mama moved in and tried to pin him against her breast. "You've got to tell us where you got that money, dear," she said. "We'll see that you don't get into trouble, but you've got to tell us the truth."

With all of us crowded into the bathroom, there was hardly room to move; the air was still steamy from Brother's bath but nobody thought to get out. Brother backed away from Mama, bumped into Daddy. Daddy sat down suddenly on the toilet seat and stayed there looking constipated. Mama maneuvered around to get another bear-hug on Brother but he stiff-armed her away. "You had no right to look in that wallet," he countered. "I didn't steal that money and as for anything else, it's none of your business.

For Crissake, I'm not a snot-nosed kid." (I took that as aimed at me in the doorway.) I could tell what was coming. Brother would work himself into a rage, the way a girl would break down in tears, to ward off a showdown. "You've got to stop spying on me, you hear? Asking who is it, before you call me to the telephone. Straightening out my bureau drawers—straightening out, I *bet*! Looking into my wallet. You've got to stop it, you'd better leave me alone, you hear?"

I didn't intend to say anything. Let him get out of this himself, I thought with tight-lipped satisfaction. I could clear him with one word, just like that, but that word would not come from me. But then I saw Mama crying, tears running down the deep lines beside her nose like water carving canyons in desert rocks.

"He didn't steal it, Mama," I said, "truly he didn't." They all looked at me, but it was Brother's look that held me. He was flushed pink from his bath, his damp hair still held the wave he had set in it, he looked clean and fresh and more handsome than I had ever noticed. But his big blue eyes looked at me and I could see him killing me and coming in to take another bath and looking just as clean and fresh and handsome. When they questioned me, I swore loyally that I just knew Brother wouldn't steal, that was all. Which made Mama pick me up to hug and cry against, choking with endearments.

In the end they had to pretend to believe him—that he had saved it up from his caddying tips. I knew one thing: whatever Brother had done, it must have been worse than stealing. I didn't want to know more. I stopped spying on him (for the same reason, I suppose, Mama stopped snooping). But it was too late. Without knowing what the crime was, knowing only its enormity, I felt trapped by complicity, gagged by my own guilt.

Every day, walking home from school, I looked up at the Pen at the top of the hill, so conveniently located, just a matter of time. At night, the lights to which I had long been accustomed awoke me now, and I would lie still in the darkness, holding my breath until the beam passed my window, passed Brother's window, once more around without having discovered where we lay.

I never did tell. I remember evenings that winter when we were all in the living room. I would be sitting at a table doing homework, and Brother would be sprawled on the floor in front of the radio listening to Gangbusters or some program like that. Daddy would be listening too, but hidden in the old wing-back chair, only the smoke rings he liked to blow signaling his presence. Mama.—well, Mama would be wearing her reading glasses, poring over the real estate section in the paper (she liked to read the descriptions of mansions for sale in the exclusive neighborhoods of the city), sitting close to the fire to toast her feet, which were always cold. Every now and then she would look up at us, pushing the glasses onto her forehead, first checking to see if I was working on my lessons, then looking at Brother, love licking at her face as unevenly as the firelight. It was then I would think about telling. Just think about it. It was like that rock, scissors, paper game that Brother used to play with me as an excuse for whacking me hard when I lost. Hands behind the back and at a sign, throw out a fist (rock) or two fingers (scissors) or an open palm (paper). Rock breaks scissors, scissors cuts paper, and paper covers rock. Brother was scissors, mother was rock. If I spoke up (forgetting that scissors would cut me into little bits), paper would cover rock. I played that game over and over in my mind, watching Mama watch Brother, but I never spoke up.

It was to happen almost like that anyway, although I had never pictured scissors defeating rock. In his last year of high school, Brother met a pretty Irish girl, from a family Mama at her kindest called "low-down." They were married almost overnight. Brother dropped out of school, got a job as trucker's helper with Railway Express and had a new baby every year. After that, whenever I saw him, he was drinking beer. He blew up like a balloon, revealing the porcine quality that had always underlain his good looks. In the only snapshot of him I have, taken just before I left home, he looks like a pig. And I think back to how he was a god to Mama, and to me a shining Lucifer, and how he failed us both.

After that, Mama changed. She closed out the family the way Daddy had closed out many a business—cleared the shelves, paid off debts outstanding (when I left home, she cried a little), then locked the doors. I have come back a few times, Brother more often, living so close, both alone and with his wife and many children, but the doors don't open. They made a little money during the war—who didn't?—and she plays the stock market. She has a kind of formal camaraderie with her broker and spends her mornings in one of those offices walled in from the street by dark green glass, where the ticker tape is screened. The people sit on seats in rows, get up and walk around, sit again, like passengers in a tight green-walled ship confined to aimlessness while hurling through space toward a far-off but quite definite destination. Afternoons she sleeps, leaving Daddy ambling through the house with a forlorn stoop, the erstwhile "worried family man" now unemployed, like an old vaudeville star who could not make it on the new silver screen.

"*Your* family," my husband snorts. "You and your brother never even write." Which is true. Not for us the pallid middle distance of mere acquaintance. Mama writes—not often, not on any set occasion, when she feels up to it. Her letters are copied studiously like homework. Sometimes, in my belated reply, I add a postscript: How is Brother getting along? And I suppose, calling her, he says when the conversation flags, "What do you hear from Sister?" And Mama writes, like a disinterested neutral interpreter, weaving back and forth between two hostile states, Brother says to tell you...And I answer, Give Brother my best.

SISTERS

THEY LIVED ALONE WITHIN TWO CITY BLOCKS OF EACH other, although the younger's rent-controlled apartment, occupied under false pretenses for so long that she no longer feared eviction, could have easily accommodated her recently widowed sister, as the younger had stressed when she made the offer, nostalgic for the Siamese-twin closeness of their youth which the elder's marriage had acted upon like a surgeon's knife, severing them from their joined past, from the earliest sharing of the same bed, the inheritance of school notes and teacher expectations, the teen-age double-dating, the pooling of costume jewelry, the midnight raillery at over-presumptuous suitors, the darker comradeship of orphans' grief in their first shared apartment.

Now, the wheel having turned full circle, came the chance to reincarnate their sisterhood in another shared apartment and yet the offer was firmly rejected by the elder, her own nostalgia centering on the heady sense of freedom she had felt when, on her honeymoon, she was more aware of the absence of her sister than the presence of her husband and realized she could use the obligations of marriage to relieve herself of the more onerous ones imposed by familial love. Not to mention (which she never did, even to herself) the relief of being removed from the ambit of the younger's beauty with which she had been in arduous competition all her girlhood, attempting to diet her stocky frame into the younger's slimness, using fake lashes as thick and furry as the younger's real ones, dyeing her carroty hair an even darker black than the rich sable shock she envied (with the unfortunate effect of making her look far more than two years older), lacquering over her freckled ruddiness with expensive makeup to achieve an unconvincing pallor, confining her breasts (an embarrassment of riches) within "minimizer" bras while the younger pranced about the apartment in nothing but a long tee shirt with no sign of bouncing. And greatest relief of all, to have found a mate who had no eye for beauty— one had only to look at his terrible ties, the outrageous colors of his socks (salmon, kelly green, royal blue) and the sad pastels of wash-and-wear-wrinkled shirts to know that he was "tone-deaf" to any aesthetic values—and who did not seem to even notice when she subsided into her natural coloring and allowed the matronly figure stenciled in her genes to take form, a matter of "settling down" as she conceived it, inextricably linked to buying a small frame house in the suburbs and bearing two children and learning to cope alone with plumbing leaks and furnace failures and weedy lawns and the constant break-down of second-hand cars that was her lot as the wife of a union organizer as much on the road as any traveling salesman, even as she worked part-time at the public library and volunteered for the League of Women Voters, Amnesty International and Save the Children Federation and still found enough parts of time to man the phones and lick the envelopes for any left-wing third-party candidate who succeeded in getting on the ballot. And when by slow degrees the children had melted away to lead foreign lives in far-off places, leaving little trace beyond a few pieces of scarred furniture, high-school yearbooks, a drawerful of baseball cards which her son had once forbidden her to throw away because they might be valuable some day, the old upright piano on which her daughter had learned to play, too ugly to sell, too costly to cart away, she had suffered only the mildest sense of loss, easily accommodating to their absence, rediscovering the freedom from familial obligations, much as she had entered into menopause with hardly a hot flash noted, relieved to be done with that monthly reminder of the obligations of her sex.

It was the younger who all those years had clung to sisterhood, using as excuse her brother-in-law's frequent absences to invite herself for weekends, bent on assuaging an abandoned wife's loneliness (however bravely denied), bringing unsuitable toys for the children (recommended by the manufacturer for ages two to six, then six to twelve, then twelve to adult, but always long outgrown by niece and nephew), disturbing the orderliness of the house with cigarette ashes and the leprous mark of forgotten drinks on Danish teak, corrupting the Ivory-soap purity of the bathroom with her array of samples from expensive cosmetic houses, slicking the tub with scented bath oil, breaking the Sunday peace with incessant chatter about lovers and jobs, both of which changed (in particulars, not in essence) with such regularity that the elder abandoned all effort at keeping up and only half-listened to the obsessive recounting of firings and betrayals, content to discern through all the chatter a similar pattern of failure both in a career that followed the punctuated theory of evolution, with sharp breaks rather than a gradual upward progress, changes from one job to another, one field to another, and in a love life showing the same abrupt disconnections, sudden sweeping extinctions. Harder to endure were the remembrances of time past invoked by those confidences, so like the late-night sessions of their girlhood when she had been forced to listen to amorous adventures for which she could provide no counterpart, shrinking before the invidious comparison made by the long door mirror in the small bedroom they had shared, clasping hands behind head to lift ponderous breasts (each like a cow's udder with only one teat) as she watched the other dress for a date, hooking a tiny wisp of lacy bra around small firm cones that needed no support at all.

On special occasions—the fourth of July barbecue in the backyard, the Christmas tree trimming, the children's birthdays—when the family's self-image required the presence of a husband and forbade the wandering-off of the children and, weather permitting, flushed out the husband's old parents from the distant farm upstate, there was less opportunity for the sibling intimacies the elder found so wearing, protected as she was by the fullness of the house, the mix of young and old voices, the comings and goings up and down the stairs, in from and out to the yard, herself so busy with basting the turkey and toning down the hyperactivity of the children and overseeing her husband's performance as host (he was apt to forget to pass around the crackers and mashed sardines or to refill his parents' glasses with ginger ale when he fixed the younger another gin and tonic) that the visit passed without need for any communication, only a quick squeeze of the younger's thin arm in a Morse code of emotion as they said goodbye on the suburban train platform conveying the fondness that swept over her at the moment of departure, made piquant by the pity that formulated itself into Scripture: what doth it profit a woman to be born a beauty if she never marry?

The squeeze, rubbing muscle against bone, could be painful but the younger treasured it as evidence of the one enduring relationship that neither time nor custom could stale, grounded in crib memories of being tickled on bare belly until she cried for surcease, of bright-colored toys held out then withdrawn just out of reach, of watching in the mirror her thick hair (thick even at birth, her mother boasted) pulled into crazy clumps and tied with grosgrain ribbons only to be painfully jerked off along with a few strands of hair and tied again in a different design, of being held and fondled and talked to like a doll in paroxysms of play that stopped as suddenly as they began, leaving her asprawl on the floor, abandoned for real playmates calling from outdoors

Toddling after, running after, never catching up until the seven-car pile-up on the icy road made them instant orphans, the two years between them moot now that they were contemporaries in grief and guilt and fear that felt as binding as any blood tie but which dissipated soon enough once they had moved from the tree-shadowed, lawn-aproned house of their parents and signed their first apartment lease in the nearby megacity, a momentous act signifying adulthood (although only the elder's name was legally valid), leaving behind the furniture of childhood and plotted suburban space for the cramped quarters of a renovated railroad flat which, aside from the provision of hot water and heat, remained much the same as its first immigrant inhabitants had found it a century earlier, its box-car alignment of closet-sized rooms, ventilated by an airshaft, terminating in one somewhat larger whose windows opened onto the street with a view of crumbling tenements across the way and below a dreary mix of down-and-outers recognizable immediately as "bums" and the work-weary, age-worn relics from the neighborhood's Ukranian past—the women waddling by on swollen ankles and overturned

heels, the men, bull-necked and shoulder-humped, cling-
ing to the rumpled self-importance of ancient double-
breasted suits.

To the younger this was but one of the myriad sights
of a city lifted from the Arabian Nights, full of magic
and exotic creatures and eye-opening adventures to which
she gave herself without reservation, confident that every
stranger she met would turn out to be a poet or an artist or
something in the theater or, at worst, a fabulously rich ty-
coon for whom making money was in itself an art form,
confident too that the elder, grumble as she might about
grime and garbage, was equally enchanted with their new
life together and the close intimacy of crowding each other
before the one mirror to put on morning makeup, of returning home after the day's work to jostle each other at
the small stove and laundry-tub of a sink while recounting
what had happened on the job and where they had shopped
at lunch, discussing how to save enough for a really grand
vacation (Italy! Italy! was their joint sigh), then facing the
more immediate problem of what to wear for a weekend
date—a problem more often pressing for the younger since
these were the days when the hegemony of her beauty was
established and nothing was denied her, no job she applied
for but she was hired, no taxi she hailed that did not screech
to a stop, no porter she needed who did not immediately
materialize, no stranger she approached when lost who did
not go out of his way to direct her, no repair required in the
apartment but the janitor, though floating among several
buildings, was there to fix it—a time the younger was al-

ways to remember as the halcyon days of their kinship, destroyed by that most unpredictable event, the elder's marriage.

The thirty years that passed counted as nothing: the younger was convinced that, with widowhood, the companion of her youth was at last restored to her, preferring to attribute the remoteness that had grown between them to a husband—but now he was dead—and to children— but they had disappeared, the boy having buried himself in an ashram somewhere in India, seeking the kind of enlightenment his parents showed no tolerance for (a cop-out from the real problems of the world, in their parlance), and the girl an even worse blow to their proletarian sympathies, married to a French businessman (no doubt needed as back-up to her career as a high-fashion model) with a tile-roofed house in Neuilly-sur-Seine that looked like a Mediterranean villa and a Mediterranean villa built of concrete and glass, photographs of which she had sent her parents (but none of herself and new husband, at least none the younger had been shown), such identification with houses seemingly a genetic trait already evidenced by a photograph the younger still possessed of her own parents in proprietary pose before their ranch-style house, on which the lens had focused with the meticulous clarity of a real-estate brochure, registering every detail from the vase of gladioli in the picture window to the side portico sheltering a fin-backed car, while allowing the human figures to be subsumed in the glare of the sun—a pose repeated by their elder daughter on the Christmas card she had made, showing her and her husband, flanked by the boy and girl, in front of their one-and-a-half story house (full attic converted to a bedroom for the children), the Christmas spirit expressed more by the house itself, its door emblazoned with a huge holly wreath and twin spruces on either side festooned with tiny cone-shaped lights than by the huddled forms and shadowed faces under hooded parkas meant to convey a family lined up in holiday greeting but to the younger more like a family evicted into the winter cold, a family doomed moreover never to find another shelter since year after year the same card was sent, the spruces the same height, the children the same ages— the girl a sulky fifteen already feeling superior to all her blood kin by virtue of her long legs and bone-sharp beauty, with something awkward about the way her hand was held in mother's grasp, more as restraint than in affection, as if force were required to pull her into the frame of the picture, and the boy at thirteen offering more passive resistance, head bowed in contemplation of his gaping untied shoes, hands fisted into the kangaroo pocket of his jacket, stooping under the weight of his father's arm thrown over his shoulders—although it had to be admitted he stooped that way even when not so encumbered and always walked with eyes directed at his feet as if their placement one after the other required strict supervision. It gave the younger what she called "the willies" to see them for so many Christmases still standing there even after they had gone their separate and distant ways, the same clutch at the heart she had when, riffling through her mail, she came upon a letter addressed to her last lover, still the titular lessee of the apartment but dead now for more than two years, usually from the Canadian or Hong Kong or Australian lottery which he was wont to enter when disgusted with his luck at home (once a gambler, always a gambler, was the conviction these persistent attempts betrayed), or from Newsweek saluting him as one of their most intelligent, well-informed readers, therefore this gentle reminder, re-reminder, re-re-reminder that his subscription had expired.

It was a terrible thought to have at her brother-in-law's graveside, and the younger mentally slapped herself for it, feeling all the more ashamed for her tepid grief, as tepid as her liking for the man when alive, a man who showed no passion except for workers and their ilk (a category into which she somehow failed to fall although she had worked for her living all her adult life), but there it was: there'll have to be a new card now, one can't send greetings from the dead. A facile weeper, she had learned long ago the trick of allowing tears to well up, adding a gem-like sparkle to periwinkle-blue eyes without the overflow that would smear mascara and eyeliner, so that, as the first shovel of dirt fell on the coffin, she saw the elder through a watery shimmer as her own true sister in a Lazarus-like revival, cured of the petulance of marriage and the distractions of motherhood, just the two of them again—a vision barely disturbed by the presence of the daughter, flying in and out on the Concorde, having just time enough in a busy schedule to model grief in a long black skirt and swallow-tail three-quarter-length coat, her blouse a furious ruffle of white organdy from which the stalk of a neck rose as from a lily pad (the son was absent, unlocatable even by the consul in Madras, his last known port of call).

Fat chance, no way, not on your life, the elder privately swore, so repulsive was the thought of moving in with the younger, no escape from that everlasting chatter, doing everything *together* (little sister always asking where she was going, always asking could she come too)—a vision of their future as a reprise of their past that sent a great *no!* exploding within her, after which there was such a fall-out of guilt as to be her undoing had she not lit upon the younger's illegal tenancy as justification for her refusal and, to buttress her need for greater security than such a precarious tenancy offered, even applying to herself that demeaning epithet, senior citizen, (a category the younger would have no truck with, forgoing all discounts offered by merchants, still paying full fare on the buses and at the movies). She went so far as to hold out the possibility, merely hinted at, carefully left unspoken, that she might find for herself an apartment large enough to accommodate the younger—a possibility she could safely discount, knowing that the younger would never abandon the rambling old apartment of her late lover, to whom she regarded herself as good as married and therefore due all the rights of inheritance had not death taken him by surprise and unfortunately intestate, leading to the discovery that his ex-wife was not officially an ex as was made clear by that lady's invasion of the premises and the removal of such valuables as caught her eye, including the Navajo rug, the Mexican hand-blown glasses, the two Picasso prints, although she was generous enough to leave behind the roomful of her husband's crated unsold books, snatched from the jaws of fire at the hands of his feckless publishers, nor did she contest the occupancy of the apartment, not on the side of town she now preferred to live in.

Guilt had much to answer for, the elder was to discover, since it was guilt, still unassuaged, that drove her to take an apartment in the same neighborhood—a small one, to be sure, with only one bedroom, close but not too close, separate but not too far apart—although it took some weeks for the consequences to be felt, her first reaction being satisfaction with the modest rent and the amenities provided by urban life as well as the stimulation of a rich ethnic mix that supported such a variety of shops—from bodegas to gourmet delis, from bargain stores with their goods spilling out on the street to small reclusive boutiques, from cosmopolitan coffee houses with outdoor tables of wrought iron painted white under large umbrellas bearing the names of French aperitifs to cheap restaurants whose decor was formica and fluorescence and whose menu was a hash of Chinese and Cuban, to all of which the younger introduced her with the grand manner of a seigneur showing off the riches of his demesne, bypassing the lower orders to formally present the newcomer to the manager or the owner with whom she seemed on the most intimate of terms, inquiring about the wife's gallstone operation or the children's schooling or the difficulties with immigration or the latest venture in real estate—an intimacy that extended even to those homeless beggars who had established a regular station outside the bank, the supermarket and the cinema, profitable locations all, chosen to imbue the exiting patrons with guilt for their access to a machine that spewed out money, for their shopping bags filled with food, for their wasteful expenditure on an evening's entertainment, a stratagem that left the elder unmoved since she disapproved of capitalistic entrepreneurship at any level and preferred to give her contributions (generous ones) to organizations that attacked the very roots of such problems, unlike the younger who always carried a pocketful of quarters to plop into every paper cup extended to her, along with intrusive personal advice (or so the elder saw it) to stop smoking and forgo franks and jelly doughnuts for whole-grain muffins and fresh vegetables at a salad bar.

All very well, this initial introduction to the neighborhood, but thus identified as the younger's sister, she was expected to share the same interest in every shopkeeper's personal history, to listen to interminable stories about a power outage or a parking ticket or the garage-collection racket when all she wanted was a pound of coffee ground to her specifications, and worse, to share with them *her* personal history, to which they must have been made privy by the younger as betrayed by their questions: had she finally heard from her son (no), was that really her daughter's picture on the cover of Elle (yes), had she much trouble selling her house in this depreciated market (yes), was she really planning a vacation trip to Italy (admittedly this learned not from her sister but from the brochure still in hand just picked up at the agency next door), and what a pity she hadn't come five minutes earlier, she had just missed her sister, to which her reply was almost a snort, since it seemed to her she never missed her sister, they were always running into each other on the street, which entailed standing on the curb for an hour, shifting her bags from hip to hip, while the younger recounted the minutes of last night's tenants meeting or extolled the virtues of a new health food or delivered a verbatim report of a long-distance call from some old lover who had ditched her long ago but who when sufficiently drunk still made maudlin contact by telephone, added to which there were the morning "dates" for cappuccino at the coffee house, and then the evening telephone calls (the elder had been adamant about no dropping in without ringing first) to coax her to see the movie at the neighborhood cinema or to ask for the use of her sewing machine or permission to drop off some fresh basil picked up at the farmers' market or to describe in soporific detail what the elder dismissed as the Pain of the Week—stiffness at the back of her neck (meningitis?), an ache in her wrist (carpal tunnel syndrome?), a sudden onslaught of fatigue (Lyme disease?), a new brown spot on her cheek (melanoma?), for all of which the elder could have provided the more dire prognosis of simple aging but with a sense of great forbearance merely rested the phone on her shoulder, allowing that little-girl voice that had never developed an adult timbre to become a background buzz while she watched TV with the sound turned down and grunted well-timed monosyllables to confirm that the connection still held, not even bothering to counter with her own aches and pains, particularly the gnawing one at the back of her shoulder (bursitis?). Only the afternoons were safe havens from her sister's intrusion, since she was occupied from one to five with her volunteer work for the city testing for racial discrimination in certain landlords' renting practices and the younger, although officially retired, worked those same hours as a sales clerk in a small lingerie shop, where she was paid "off the books" thereby enabling her to retain her full social security payments and which she pressed the elder to patronize, touting the owner as one of a vanishing breed, like stone-masons, fine furniture craftsmen or watch repairers—in this case, a real corsetiere who knew how to mold even the fullest figure into fashionable proportions— but the elder, having long since lost interest in her breasts, considered she had done her duty by them in choosing a surplice neckline on all her dresses.

Chattering away, cajoling, presenting little gifts (fresh herbs from the farmer's market, earrings from a street vendor, a jar of all-natural eucalyptus oil to rub on that aching shoulder, unspoken of but not unnoticed), the younger felt the sting of every rejection, unspoken but not unnoticed, yet having been accused of paranoia by so many lovers, took herself in hand, using the same contemptuous voice of rationality those very lovers had assumed in dismissing her suspicions (all of which proved true): it was just her imagination that the elder, seeing her two blocks away, had crossed to the other side of the street to avoid her (for one thing, her sister's eyesight had never been that good), nor did it mean much that all their conversations were so one-sided (her sister had always been the quiet one), and on those mornings they met for coffee, that constant checking of the time need be no indication of boredom but merely a busier schedule than the younger set for herself, besides which the poor girl (to the younger they were forever girls) was still suffering from her recent loss and when in pain had always withdrawn into herself, just as the younger had always talked her out of it and was determined to do so now, shrugging off the minor rebuffs (like water off a duck's back, she congratulated herself) until that day she entered the gourmet deli for her special blend of coffee and received a blow that stunned her into silence, for what was there to say to the news (presented not as news, of course, to one so close as a sister) that the elder would soon be off to Italy. To Italy, to Italy, was all her dazed mind could grasp, the Italy on which their youthful fantasies had been fixed, as if the travel brochures and guides to and books about and maps spread on the bed were all the decoration their dingy apartment required—a trip planned with ever-changing itineraries to encompass every Tuscan village or Calabrian outpost mentioned in the travel section of the Sunday Times, and for which they were still saving up when the elder so suddenly chose to marry. And now so suddenly chose to carry out alone, the news delivered in this back-door way by the deli owner as he ground the coffee beans to order, dealing a pain as stabbing sharp as the "stitch in the side" of her childhood when in pursuit of her sister she had run too fast, too long along the winding suburban street, in and out of neighbors' yards, crying wait for me, wait for me.

When later that morning she passed the elder on the street, she gave the barest hello, signing with a brusque wave of the hand that she was much too busy to stop and talk (cold comfort to register her sister's shock), nor did she telephone that evening or the next or the next, waiting for the other to make the call as surely she must do before she left (who else was there to take in her mail, to water her plants?), fabricating the conversation in advance (the elder's feeble excuses, her own dignified response) so that she felt fully prepared when the call finally came, her sister as usual identifying herself by name as if the younger would not know immediately who it was, except this time there might have been some doubt, so strained, so forced was the voice the elder laid claim to, causing her own throat to constrict in reflexive fear, a cinematic disaster unrolling before her eyes (without even a goodbye, her sister leaves for Italy on a plane, which crashes—no, is hijacked), so where, she asks, is the elder calling from, is taken aback that it should be St. Barnabas, which strikes her (the catastrophe film still in play) as off-route, surely somewhere in the Caribbean? and only when the elder adds a room number does she remember St. Barnabas is a hospital on the other side of town. But still, compared to her prevision of disaster, it does not sound so alarming as she listens to the symptom that brought the elder there— the pain in the back of the shoulder that kept getting worse, in spite of the eucalyptus oil she rubbed on—here the voice takes on an accusatory tone and the younger, on the defensive, tartly agrees it was wise to take care of the problem before embarking on a long trip (this said bitterly, making it clear that all was known) although had she been consulted she would have recommended acupuncture. For breast cancer? the elder asks, outdoing her in bitterness.

Metastasized to the bone, the doctor told the younger, having come upon her at the nurses' station where she had stopped to ask directions—hopeless, the younger knew from his shifty look, although the word was carefully avoided, yet in this small conference room, at this table where residents and interns sat in judgment, the pleadings of patients reduced to files dry as lawyers' briefs, she employed her most beseeching look from eyes still periwinkle blue, which had served her so well when she was young and even now might have swayed a jury but not a hanging judge like this, who talked of calcium levels and CAT scans and how extensive was the spread, ruling out surgery, leaving only chemo combined with radiation to be tried (the tone of his voice conveying how little faith he had in that), put it in the record that he always leveled with his patients but it was bad medicine to extinguish hope and so advised her to play along with this trip to Italy her sister was so set on, let her believe it was merely postponed, after which he awkwardly took her hand, gave it a layman's helpless pat— how else to respond to that look?—pointed out the room she wanted and left her in the corridor feeling tricked, manipulated, confused, weighed down by guilt—had he not told her the elder was dying, had she not given her informed consent?

She found the elder huddled in a chair, shivering in the blue-sprigged hospital gown, while her bed was being made by a blue-coated nurse's aide, with so animated a conversation ongoing between the two that the younger's greeting, forceful in its cheerfulness, was brushed aside and, her presence acknowledged only with a hushing frown, she was reduced to watching in silence the quick skillful movements of the aide's dark hands as they tugged and smoothed the white sheets, the soft lilting Caribbean voice making a list of union grievances sound like poetry, the elder's right-on caws of support turning it into familiar prose, until finally the bed was made, the basket emptied of its tissues, the night table cleaned, the elder tucked back under the clean sheets, the blanket pulled over her, the pillows plumped behind her, the aide sent on her way with a lavishly grateful acknowledgement of services rendered, allowing the younger to draw up a chair, determined to be not only cheerful but more useful than any nurse's aide (particularly one threatening to go on strike), the gush of her assurances undeterred by the "leave-me-alone" compression of her sister's lips, the meanness in her eyes, this being nothing more than the sweetly familiar hurt of childhood—she the younger, teased and tweaked and pushed away and run from—that she had sucked on all her life, leaving her well adapted to endure in the days that followed the elder's querulous complaints, exigent demands, while the nurses, the aides, the residents, the technicians, even the man who came daily to roll the elder away on the gurney were treated with an almost obsequious politeness, thus establishing the reputation of a model patient, just as in childhood she had wooed those playmates from outside, reserving for the younger all her rage.

The daughter flew in, fidgeted at the bedside, searched for the umpteenth time for the plane ticket to Italy her mother accused the staff of stealing, interrogated the doctors, made arrangements with Social Services, grumbled at a brother so conveniently unlocatable, and two days later left the younger with a heart-felt shrug, power of attorney, and her schedule for the next few weeks—her departure unnoticed by the elder, now encapsulated in her pain like a lone traveler in space, reporting back to earth over light-years of distance through a burst of static in which occasionally some other voice comes through urging her to eat—a typical foolishness that enables her to recognize the younger, who cannot see that when the pain comes, she must give it her full attention like an infant at breast, and who so foolishly—how like the younger—cries out Nurse! as if that were not what she was doing with all her strength, giving nurse, then footsteps, one of the white-garbed myrmidons who control this terrifying place, doling out a punishment of pills, until at last the sharp-toothed suckling creature is satiated, falls asleep, leaving her free to drift weightless in cold space, cold, cold—another blanket please, someone calls for, and she clings to that frail communication with Mission Control which reaches her in the voice of the younger, to whom she tries to describe the view of earth from so far away and to deliver a message for mankind on what has gone wrong—too much competition, cutting each other dead, when what is needed is understanding, soft persuasion, living together in peace— but someone else has taken over the controls, a man's voice issuing nonsense orders and she cries aloud for her sister who alone can decipher the code.

Electrolyte imbalance, the doctor murmurs to the nurse—the confusion is transient, a common side-effect of the drugs, he reassures the younger, who therefore sees no need to telephone the daughter, who would not even recognize her mother in this withered husk, the hair grown back white, the too too solid flesh melted away, nor would her presence mean much to the elder (only the younger does she still recognize, call by name)—such is the argument the younger uses to postpone a repeat of that earlier whirlwind visit which she had found a disturbing irritant, like an anachronism in an otherwise engrossing historical drama—and having rid the tale now drawing to an end of all extraneous characters, the younger settles herself to watch by the bedside, as she does every evening until the curfew for visitors forces her to leave, the companion of her youth at last restored to her, just the two of them again, orphans afresh, cleaving to each other.

MOTHER

IT WAS LATE AFTERNOON OF AN OVERCAST DAY WHEN Joel was to meet his mother for the first time. The arrangement was of her making—4 p.m., December 3, on the steps of the library (the one building she was sure she could find, she had confided over the phone). Granted it was the usual campus meeting place for friends, classmates, student demonstrations, rock sessions, and religious revivals, it was hardly the site he would have chosen for this particular encounter.

As he approached along one of the brick-paved paths, the west facade of the library was suddenly transmuted to pure gold and he blinked, almost stumbled on the herringbone brick, for a moment as disoriented as if he had just been "beamed up" by that Star Trek device and his molecules had not quite reassembled. This was no longer the familiar campus for which, as a senior, he already felt a nostalgic affection, but a stage set on which the curtain had just risen—some luminous Venetian scene painted by a Turner—demanding instant applause even before the action started. Although he understood how it was worked—the sun, before setting, had found a hole in the clouds, that was all—the magic did not dissipate. Hit broadside by the long horizontal rays, the domed building had become a Doge's palace, so sharply outlined in its effulgent glow as to seem a two-dimensional backdrop, while still lowering overhead was the slate-colored batting of a sky, like those dark upper reaches filled with spider walks and sandbags and ropes—all the heavy machinery needed to produce such a fantasy on stage.

How like this woman to enter his life under such stagey lighting, Joel thought, crediting her with yet another special effect. Had not her letter arrived precisely on his twenty-first birthday? And ordinary mail, not express. How she had contrived that he couldn't guess, mail delivery to his dorm being what it was. Then her telephone call—on the stroke of midnight. Literally on the stroke. "Hello," he had said and the bells from the campanile began to toll. And between the letter and the call, just enough time for her story to be confirmed.

The call to his father was supposed to be brief: how long should it take to say "the woman's crazy?" Instead there was a barrage of temporizing questions—"Is this the first letter you've received? How did she get your address? Have you said anything to your mother? Does she mention what her name was before she married this guy Bernstein? Well, at least she married within her faith, your mother advised her to"—before his father said, reprovingly at that, this was not the kind of thing to discuss on the phone.

~~

An orderly man, his father realigned the silverware, the wine glass and water goblet as he always did in a restaurant. Joel knew better than to speak while he was studying the menu. "First, I'd like to see that letter," he said, as if ordering an appetizer. Joel slapped it down on his plate with the flourish of a process-server.

Without touching it, his father sighed "My God" softly. "That handwriting—I'd know it anywhere. Those fat straight up-and-down letters, circles for dots—my God, after all these years."

The faint smile of nostalgic recall told Joel all he needed to know but still he pressed, "Aren't you going to read it?"

"I was just thinking of your—of Mary," his father said, putting on his glasses. "She used to try to write like that. Then she switched to a backward slant—like a leftie, you know—" all the while he was skimming swiftly the three sheets, front and back—"she was always trying to write like somebody else, I was kinda glad when she settled for the typewriter. Although she still keeps trying out different fonts, you know?"

Ignoring Joel's "I know, I know," he carefully replaced the sheets in the envelope, slid it back across the table and resumed his reading of the menu. Joel wanted to sock him.

"Well?" Joel prompted through gritted teeth, once the ordering was accomplished.

As if only then aware of impending mayhem, his father threw up a hand defensively. "Okay, okay, it's true enough. Of course she's colored it to make herself look good, I suppose that's only natural. What you have to understand is, at that point in time, your moth—Mary and I—"

Again that stutter, wiping out his kinship. When he was little his father, returning home, would lift him high and squeeze hard. Too hard. Joel felt now that same crushing pressure around his chest.

"—I guess her not being able to have children was more upsetting than I realized," his father was saying. "All I knew was that she had become very hard to live with, always complaining, finding fault, never satisfied. I'm not the kind of guy who plays around, I want you to know that, son, I'm really—"

"I know, I know," Joel said quickly. He did not want to hear what kind of a guy his father really was.

"The fact is, she kinda drove me to it. So that when this Ella came on to me—"

A long caesura. His father was not a man to talk with his mouth full. He had large white teeth that projected in an ogive arch (there but for the grace of orthodonture, Joel never failed to think when watching him eat), and the only time his mouth was completely closed was at times such as this, when chewing became its sole function, performed with the efficiency of one of those machines in his paper mill—cutting, grinding, tonguing, pulping, all the while bathing the fibers in a wash of enzymatic fluids. At last the pulverized mass slipped down his gullet and with a recapitulating "well" he picked up the thread of his story.

"These things do happen, you know. And to be fair to *her*—" he nodded at the envelope which still lay between them as if it contained the cremated ashes of this *her*—"she was having a rough time too. She had just broken off with some guy who wanted her to give up her career and follow him behind the Bamboo Curtain. Personally I thought it was good riddance—only a commie could have gotten into China then—" his father halted the dismemberment of broiled chicken to look at him uncertainly—"this was before Nixon opened things up, it sure as hell wasn't on the tourist track—"

"I know, I know," Joel muttered, it being what he always said when his father started to explain anything. "What kind of career?"

"She was a singer. In supper clubs. Not your ordinary blues and ballads stuff—a musical satirist, I guess you'd call her. Terrific range. She'd mimic a Wagnerian soprano and have you rolling in the aisles, then she'd take off on a French diseuse or some pop star—God, she was funny!" he groaned, a man remembering the exhaustion of laughter. "My favorite was her Hildegarde number—a dame pretty hot on the supper-club circuit then, whose signature was these long white gloves she wore up to her armpits. Well, Ella'd start drawing one of them off, keep pulling, pulling, only there was no end to them and by the time she had finished the song, she would be tripping over yards and yards of the stuff, fighting with it like it was some enormous white boa constrictor—" What had begun as a low chuckle was now a paroxysmic coughing fit. Sobering up, his father said, "To remember that—after all these years."

"Is that all you remember?" Joel asked, a nasty edge to his voice.

"Oh, I remember the letter she wrote, telling me she was pregnant and intended to have an abortion."

More chewing. Joel fixed his eyes on his plate, all his concentration on his food, the look of his steak, rarer than he had ordered, and as he sliced it, how the blood still exuded from the flesh of an animal so long dead.

"Of course Mary found the letter. I must say her reaction surprised me, you never can tell with women. She was the one who talked Ella into having the child and letting us adopt it."

"I see," Joel said, deciding he was not hungry. "What they call today a surrogate mother."

His father nodded, wiped his mouth thoroughly, cleansing it for a grin. "Only the way she got the stuff shot up was not so clinical."

Joel stared across the table at the man who had carried him on his shoulders, wrestled him on the floor, taught him to throw a curve ball, cut a clean line with a saw. Who also chewed like a paper mill and told coarse jokes. It was not the first time he had told himself this man could not be his father. He had had trouble defining irony in his term paper on Austen, but he knew it when he saw it. Never once had he imagined having any other mother.

"There's one thing I don't understand," Joel said. "Why the hell did you keep it a secret all this time? For Crissake, everyone knows a kid should be told if he's adopted."

That was Mary's doing, not his, his father said. Mary, Joel warned himself, not Mother. He tried out Mary in his head and felt a shiver of something deeper than muscle, deeper than bone. It was the same chill he had felt as a child when, frightened of the night sky, Mother had made him look up at the stars and said, "Those are other worlds up there."

His father was as quick with absolution as with blame. "She just wanted to spare you, son. The way she argued—"

"Mary?" Joel asked, trying the name out loud.

His father looked offended as at some liberty taken. "You know your mother—she uses logic like one of those jar openers she keeps for opening her preserves—twist, twist, and she serves you what she herself has put inside. Because I was really your father, you weren't really adopted—that's the way she saw it. As for that—" his father gave him what was no doubt intended as a reassuring smile—"the technique may have been sloppy, but the proof's iron-clad. If you ever doubt I'm your old man, just look in the mirror."

"I know, I know," Joel said. The same set of the eyes, the same broad nostrils with their baroque flare. Except for the straightened teeth, the same coarse mouth. He was doomed, imprisoned for life, the Man in the Iron Mask hearing the clang of fate.

"Now the way *I* saw it, there was no need to argue the point since Ella was as anxious to see the last of you as we were to see the last of her. Shortly before you were born, she got a letter from her boyfriend saying China had been a mistake, his breaking with her had been a mistake, he would be back as soon as he could and would she forgive him, etc." His father smote his forehead. "Bernstein! Paul Bernstein, yeah, that was his name. So she *did* marry the guy.—Anyway, the last thing she wanted was for him to find out what she had been up to while he was away— whatever revolution he had in mind, it sure wasn't the sexual one, I gathered. As a matter of fact, she was in such a hurry to get rid of the evidence before he showed up, she pushed you out two weeks ahead of schedule. I remember that because I had to light a fire under the lawyer to get the adoption papers ready for her to sign before she left the hospital. The three of us left together—the four of us, Mary holding you all wrapped up in a blanket, tight to her chest, like she was smuggling out contraband. Outside was the only awkward moment—none of us knew what to say. I put Ella in a cab, shut the door, and we all knew that was final. She never looked back, Mary said, like she was picking a fault in her, you know. That was the whole point, I told her, she's looking ahead."

~~

Well, she's looking back now, Joel had said with a bitterness that rose again in his gorge as he neared their meeting

place. With its massive columns and classic pediment in-
scribed with Great Names, approached by a wide expanse
of steps broad in tread and shallow in riser, the library was
unmistakably a temple of learning. But, from the human
litter on the steps, limbs collapsed, bodies asprawl, it would
seem that neophytes rarely made it through its bronze
doors. Joel picked his way around the students basking in
the momentary sun to reach the fur-coated figure standing by the statue of the Founder.

"I take it you are Joel?" She answered her own question
with a smile. Her lips were cracked, a patch of red hung
loose, like paint peeling off the side of a house. She bit it
off as her eyes skimmed over him head to foot. "I didn't
need to ask, really. You're the spitting image of your
father."

Too much make-up, was what Joel saw. Gave her points
for not dyeing her hair. There was a lot of it, probably once
a flaming red which had rusted more than grayed, piled on
top of her head in a fat pouf shaggy with escaping strands,
pierced by various jewel-headed pins—an architectural
structure that had much in common with a bower-bird's
nest.

Joel felt foolish, unable to think of a suitable salutation.
The conventions did not seem to apply to a stranger who
was one's mother. Pleased to meetcha? Enchanté? He
stretched his grin and held it, hoping that would do, and
sensed a certain twitchiness in her responding smile, like
the little shimmy of a cat's haunches as it readies for a
pounce. Was she really going to kiss him? Quickly he held

out his hand, shook hers vigorously. The gesture did not have the natural flow he had desired since she first had to shift a book she was holding. Limp black leather and gold lettering, closed on a red silk ribbon flagging her place. The Holy Bible. Joel was disconcerted to see such a "churchy" edition, having grown to accept as the norm the college bookstore versions, complete with book jacket and blurbs provided by the author's friends. He judged it part of her overdressing, like the no doubt endangered species of a fur.

He looked up from the book to meet her eyes. Over his shoulder the sun struck them golden too. Drooping lids gave them an oriental cast. A large fleshy woman standing as tall as he in her high-heeled boots, further aggrandized by that fur (longer-haired, more erratically spotted than the usual cat—a lynx perhaps?), hands knobby with big-stoned rings—and carrying the Holy Bible. Transposing her to the puzzle page of a children's magazine—what's wrong with this picture?—he almost laughed aloud.

Having followed his look, she seemed to share his amusement. "I know it must look funny, but I find there are so many moments that I used to waste—standing in line, waiting for a bus—which now I put to use by reading. Without a good book, I feel off-balance, like a woman without her purse." Her smile broadened. "In this case, *the* Good Book, shouldn't I say?" For a moment he was afraid she was going to lift it to her lips, but instead she opened her bag—a capacious pouch of fabric seemingly snipped out of a Persian carpet—and dropped it in. He felt greatly relieved.

Surely there was a coffee shop nearby, or, if he preferred, a bar, she suggested with a sympathetic shiver for
someone clad in denim. "Somewhere we can talk," she said,
insinuating her arm between his elbow and his ribs. Her
modestly downcast gaze, the polite complacency in her
face rewrote him into a gentleman who had offered the
support any lady would expect.

He considered several student hangouts, rejected them
as too noisy, led her instead to a chic bistro new to the
neighborhood whose front of glass brick, allowing light to
enter but barring the interior from view, provided the privacy he desired. "Rather like a bathroom window," was her
comment as he held open the door. Having settled herself
on a banquette, she glanced at the menu and raised an
incredulous brow. Wine by the glass, but only vintage stuff,
and the potato salad boasted a grating of white truffle. "My,
my," she said, "times *have* changed. When I was your age,
a boy took me out, I was lucky to get a slice of pizza."

Quickly he calculated the cash in his wallet, all but certain he had left his credit card at home. She called herself
his mother, he had assumed she would pay the check.

"I thought you wanted to talk," he said in an injured
tone, "this is the only quiet place I know."

"And a very nice place it is," she said quickly, looking about the room, empty but for two couples who had
chosen tables at a discreet distance from each other. "I like
the artwork," she said, with a nervous excess of appreciation. She even turned to follow the evenly paced array of
Georgia O'Keeffe posters. "Though I wish they weren't all

flowers—there's something ferocious about her flowers—
as if they were man-eaters."

Not much interested in art, Joel gave a cursory look to
the red poppy behind her. "I suppose they chose flowers
because that's the name of this place—Flowers."

"Oh," she said, for the first time allowing her glance
to settle on him. "Do you come here often?"

"Not often," he said. Just once, would have been more
precise. A clandestine meeting with May Toy, his room-
mate's girl, who had broached the possibility of seeing him
alone with such lascivious tittering that he had thought....
He darted a resentful look at the corner table where he had
wasted a half-hour waiting for her and twenty bucks on
patisserie, only to discover that all she wanted was advice
about computers. According to Ben, that was his field of
expertise, she had said with the same stupid titter.

His present table partner called him to order.

"You must be wondering why now, after all these
years." Less a statement than an explosion to unclog the
silence. The energy she had summoned for that effort
restored for a moment the florid coloring of youth. This,
Joel told himself, was the woman his father had once bed-
ded—this large-boned beauty with crackling hair and a
tiger's eyes. But even as he looked his amazement, the transient flush subsided, the fire was banked, the tiger tamed.

"You're twenty-one, you see. I figured my agreement
with Mary had run out. Like a statute of limitations—or is
that just with taxes?"

Joel's shrug was not helpful. He found it quite satisfy-
ing not to be helpful, to leave it all to her. But her next stab

at conversation jolted him. "You don't happen to carry a picture of Mary and your father by any chance?" His disconcerted stare told her she might as well have asked if he carried a hacksaw on his person. Defensively she insisted that people do, you know. "Carry snapshots of their nearest and dearest. I have one—" she fumbled inside the cavernous bag—"of your half-sister. Would you like to see her?"

"No," he said perversely, knowing even as he said it that the face not seen would haunt him.

Her head jerked up as if slapped. Ashamed, he grunted, oh, all right, reached across the table, but she withdrew her hand empty and squeezed his, leaving him with the feel of long nails and heavy rings and the flesh-and-blood warmth of a female stranger.

"I understand," she said, "first you and I must get to know one another. So how do we begin? This *is* embarrassing, isn't it?" She threw back her head and gave a deep-throated laugh that enabled Joel to see every gold filling in her mouth. Better that, he thought, than having to view her braless state, which he could not help but notice when she leaned forward. A gruesome scene wrote itself out: That's my mother all right, he identified the headless corpse, I can tell from that lozenge-shaped brown mark on her right breast.

Revolted by such thoughts, he resolved to meet her halfway. "You were a singer, weren't you?"

She widened her eyes in surprise. How does she do that without raising her brows, he wondered. He noticed darker flecks embedded in the amber. "How did you know? Oh.

You've spoken to your father since I called. To vet me, I suppose."

She made it sound like a breach of trust. Huffily he pointed out it was natural he should consult his father. Quite natural, she agreed. Just as it was natural for the natural mother to want to meet her natural son.

Unnatural son she might better have called him. He felt nothing for this woman. A natural curiosity, yes, but even that was fractured by two conflicting urges: the desire to know, the desire not to know. To open mouth, ask questions. To clap hands over ears, shut out the answers.

"So?" she nudged him. "What else did he say about me?"

Joel could not remember what else his father had said. As if he had clapped hands over ears in that confrontation as well.

"That you were very funny," he finally dredged up.

Chapped lips compressed into a self-deprecating grimace. "Those who can, sing. Those who can't, entertain. Oh, well, I made a good thing out of my limitations, making fun of my betters." Planting both elbows on the table, she asked, "Shall I give you a sample?"—a purely rhetorical question for she ignored his vigorous headshake and, as if in a Hollywood musical of the thirties, burst into song. Why doesn't an orchestra strike up, he wondered wildly. as her husky contralto throbbed throughout the room with a Gallic vibrato as thick as phlegm. Among his parents' collection of old 78's, there was a recording of Edith Piaf singing the same song, with her picture on the jacket, and the totally dissimilar face before him had miraculously acquired the same cavernous-eyed look of a love-battered gamine.

Sensing the startled attention of the two couples behind him, he slumped in his chair, tried to blot out the voice so authentic in its Gallic flavor and yet—he could not put his finger on what was wrong but there was something slightly off, hardly noticeable, but giving a ludicrous twist to those overly-nasal tones, making a mockery of such abandonment to love. His embarrassment was only intensified by the laughter and applause which greeted her at the end—even the kitchen staff had appeared in an inner doorway to clap appreciatively. "Oh God," he groaned when she responded by kissing both hands and flinging wide her arms.

"You see, your father was right, I *am* very funny," she said. "Of course, to really do it right, I should have gotten up and worked the tables, but I was afraid that might embarrass you."

He looked at her suspiciously. There was such a mischievous puckering about her mouth, he could not help but laugh.

"There, that's better. All over and done with," she said soothingly, as if she had just taken him to the dentist. "So is that all he said?"

"Who?" It *was* like being at the dentist. He was getting numb.

"Your father," she said impatiently. "Did he tell you that Mary and I were old high school buddies?"

He stuttered his surprise. "I thought—he didn't exactly say—but I got the impression—"

"That we were perfect strangers? Oh, no! Not that we were *ever* best friends or anything and we didn't bother to keep up with each other after graduation. But you know how it is when you're that age, you're not very happy with yourself and to rub it in, there's usually one person in your class who is everything you aren't but want to be. That was Mary, for me. Perfect hair, perfect features, perfect figure, perfect clothes, perfect manners, perfect house, perfect parents—my God, they had cocktails every night before dinner, how more perfect can you be?"

How did she do it—these transformations? Now he was facing a straight-backed, narrow-shouldered creature whose head seemed to support itself on an elongated neck, whose elbows would never rest on a table, whose knees, though hidden, were surely in polite touch with each other. It was like watching an exuberantly bushy tree being trimmed into topiary art. And then—a small movement yet shockingly at odds with that armature of formal composure—her fingers plucked the air, captured an imaginary strand of hair, placed it behind her ear, impressing on it with milking strokes the ear's curve. For the second time, he found himself laughing against his will.

"Remind you of someone?" she asked, relaxing into her own persona.

"Grandma," he said, still grinning. "To a tee."

She looked at him curiously, then shrugged. "So that's where it comes from," she said obscurely, and resumed her confessional mode. "What I didn't know at the time was that Mary felt exactly the same—I mean, she wanted to be *me*. At least that's what she said when we met again after all those years. She had read that I was singing at the Regis and dragged Ed to see me and of course I recognized her immediately. After my number I came over to their table and we got to talking and I told her about my high-school crush and she told me about hers and I couldn't believe it." She shook her head as if nothing had since happened to diminish her incredulity.

"Is that supposed to explain why you took her husband?" There was more pugnacity in the question than he had intended but she merely seemed amused.

"No-o-o." She drawled out the negative as if fully considering the suggestion. "Any more than I think that's why she took my baby."

He was thrown into painful confusion. He wasn't ready for the baby—it took him a moment to even realize who the baby was.

"Oh God! I've hurt you!" Her tragic cry resonated through the almost empty room. From the corner of his eyes, Joel saw the two waiters leaning against the bar in idle conversation jump to attention. No doubt the two parties in back of him were also awaiting further developments. "I'd rather cut out my tongue than say anything to upset you. Please, please forgive me, say you forgive me—"

"Of course I forgive you," Joel whispered, hoping to set an example. "I mean, there isn't anything to forgive, I'm not upset, believe me."

Perhaps he had spoken *too* low, she didn't seem to have heard him. "Do you think I'm exposing myself this way—" she leaned forward but Joel knew now to fix his eyes on the red poppy behind her—"just to give you pain? Maybe it was selfish, wanting to see my own child—"

"No, no, no," Joel murmured in a hushing tone and shifted his gaze from the poppy. In this woman's presence, even the private parts of a flower made him uncomfortable.

"Yes, yes, yes. Selfish, selfish, selfish." Her voice was throaty with emotion, as if she were about to render another Piaf song. Joel read her abrupt wave to the waiter as a signal of all hope abandoned. Don't, he pleaded, don't leave.

Again it was as if he had not spoken. "Another cappuccino," she ordered and as the waiter withdrew gave Joel a complicitous wink. "I'd been trying to catch his eye for the last ten minutes—"

She was harder to read than May Toy, he decided. "Anyway," he prompted after a long pause, "you and my father had this affair..."

"As is self-evident," she said, removing her elbow from the table to make room for the new cup of coffee. "But that's not what I want to explain." She ladled in a big spoonful of the cinnamon-dusted froth, leaving a rabid fringe of white foam in the corners of her mouth. "Whatever happened between Ed and me—" her hand flicked through the air, brushing away an insignificant gnat of memory—"was of no importance. He was pissed off at Mary, I was pissed off—no, I was *enraged*—at Paul, that's all."

Joel emitted a short harsh sound "I just thought of something funny. Love child—isn't that what the Victorians used to call their bastards? In my case, spite child is more like it, wouldn't you say?"

She smacked the table with her open palm. Cups danced in their saucers, his spoon tiddlewinked to the floor. "Why do you think you're the star of this production? You're not even in the cast of characters yet!" When, having picked up the spoon, he raised his flushed face above table level, he was relieved to find her tigerish gaze fixed on more distant prey. "Just like your sister, just like your sister."

"Half-sister," he felt impelled to interject.

"There's nothing half about her," was the bitter response. "Whole hog or nothing, that's her. She's *done* drugs, she's *done* sex, now she's into *doing* Jesus."

In spite of his specific denial of any interest, she was showing him that girl's picture. "I was under the impression that *you* were doing Jesus," he said resentfully.

Her look of incomprehension did not fool him for a minute. He gave a significant nod at her handbag; she could not deny she had a Bible stowed inside.

"Oh that," she said with a shrug, then stiffened with a sudden look of enlightenment. "When you first saw me, you thought that *I*—oh, that look on your face—" For a moment she was incapacitated by laughter, pulled herself together with an "oh dear, oh dear." Rather unnecessarily, he thought, she told him he did not know how funny that was. "You see, for Mary I was a mite too Jewish, for you I am a mite too Christian—it's obvious I will never get it right." He had to wait until she recovered from another bout of laughter before she told him that it was her daughter's Bible, not hers. And out of habit, she supposed—she had always checked up on her daughter's reading when she was a kid—she was skimming through it. "You know, I never read the New Testament before—it has really got some good stuff in it. No, really, I mean it." She said this so graciously, with such an approving smile at him, he was tempted to say thank you.

"Look—uh—" he began and fell into the trap he had been so skillfully avoiding. What to call her? Mrs. Bernstein, as if she were an imposter? Ella, as if she were a classmate or a girl met at a party?

Her rueful smile told him she was sensitive to his dilemma. "Call me Ella," she prompted, "my daughter does. I know that some things can't be changed—that Mary is the one you will always call mother."

He felt a skin-deep prickle over his temples as if some device were mapping his nerve endings. Mother, she was saying, was the imposter. "Okay," he said, meanly determined to call her nothing.

She waited for him to finish his thought, but he sat there like a stone. With an exasperated "oh!" she wrung her napkin as if it were a neck. "She should have told you herself. Long ago. Now it's too much of a shock."

"She wanted to spare me," he said like an automaton.

"Spare you what?" she hurled back. "The knowledge that you're half-Jewish? Well, that cat's out of the bag."

His jaw dropped. "I haven't even thought of that."

The tiger brightness of her eyes faded into the soft-focus of tears. "I'm sorry, dear. It's just that, knowing Mary, I was afraid—"

"I'll tell you what she wanted to spare me," he said fiercely, in a panic to deny her words before they were spoken. "She wanted to spare me the knowledge that you gave me away, left me just like that." He was appalled to feel the wetness in his own eyes. It must be in his blood, he thought, this staginess—this employment of high drama to conceal, to deceive. For in truth, he felt nothing. If he were to cry, it would be more for what she wanted to take away than for what she had failed to give.

"Just like that," she repeated softly enough, for which he was grateful, seeing the clenched fists, the tendons stretching out her neck. "Do you have any idea of what *that* was like? I saw you once, just once, right after you were born—a slippery monkeyish thing—and knew that if I looked again, I was lost. So I left you with those who were sure to love you—your real father and a woman who wanted to be a mother above all else. I've hated her ever since."

"You can't!" Joel said, feeling another prickle of alarm. "She's done nothing wrong, she's been—"

"She stopped me from having an abortion—that would have been a wound that time could heal. But the birth of a real child—monkeyish though it is—leaves such a hole, such a gaping hole." She groped in her bag and pulled out a crumpled wad of paper tissues. Careful of her mascara, Joel noticed, she pressed them to her lower lids to trap the overflow of tears, as if it were a cache of some magic liquor. Then with a gesture of finality gave her nose a wadded tweak. "Enough of that," she said firmly, as if disapproving of some third party's histrionics. "I do think you should know, however, that I have followed your career with great interest."

"My career?" Joel asked, astounded to hear that, his present indecision notwithstanding, he had one.

"Oh well," she said with a little laugh, "the early intimations of the one to come. You took first place at your high school science fair, didn't you? And are a National Merit Scholar. You also had the lead in your senior class play—Our Town, as I remember—but I wouldn't recommend the stage. No, you are obviously going into science and just as obviously will win a Nobel Prize."

At that moment Joel decided to take his father's advice. "Wrong, I'm going for a MBA." He closed his mouth determinedly. He would not ask. He did not want to know. "How did you know all that about me?"

"Oh, I have my sources," she said, narrowing her eyes mysteriously. "I've known every time Ed expanded his business, every time Mary took up another good cause. I've known when you had that biking accident and were hospitalized in Vermont. The girl you had a fancy for when you were fifteen. The time—"

"I'm asking how, not what," he said coldly, but the anger roiling his insides was asking, by what right?

Her eyes opened to ingenuous size. She would be frank now, they announced. "I've been a faithful subscriber to your home-town newspaper for twenty years. Then there are those high-school yearbooks. And the student newspaper from this college of your choice. You might say I've run my own clipping service."

He could not conceal his relief, having formed a nightmarish picture of a tall trench-coated figure, scarf tied babuska-fashion over a yeasty pompadour of red hair, tail-ing him through life, keeping always just beyond his peripheral vision.

She reached across the table and gave him a reassuring pat on the arm. "Don't worry, I know my place. In the wings, not on stage."

"Look—" he had remembered now what he wanted to say—"Dad feels it would be best if this were kept just between the three of us."

Her expression was one of exaggerated surprise. "I rather thought Mary already knew she was not your real mother—a woman's intuition, you know."

"I mean—"

"Oh, I know what you mean. She's not to know that you know. That's okay by me—on one condition. I want to attend your graduation, so you must see that I get an invitation, or whatever I need to get in."

Not to worry, she answered his obvious concern, she would be sure to keep out of the way. Besides, after all these years, she doubted if Mary would recognize her. Or she, Mary. Which was why she had wanted to see a picture.

"I've been trying to remember her as I last saw her—grown up, married, and all that—but the Mary I keep seeing is the one I knew in high school—" The eyes brightened, the face flushed, the words bubbled out as if memory were an alcoholic beverage on which she was getting high. She kept asking him for confirmation: did Mary still look like—? did Mary still choose clothes that—? did Mary still believe in—? did Mary still laugh at—? was Mary still offended by—?

All these "Marys" pierced him like electrodes, causing his right knee to jerk galvanically, up and down, up and down. He put his coffee down carefully to keep it from slopping over. I never noticed. I never asked. I never thought about it. I don't know. He was answering her like an indicted co-conspirator taking the fifth on the witness stand.

She must have sensed his discomfort. Or perhaps, as with any high, there was the inevitable falling off into depression. The mobile face drooped with sadness, acknowledging its age. She hardly seemed aware that he was asking for the check, although when it came she plucked it from his hand, not deigning to reply to his pro forma protest. Even during their strangely formal goodbyes, she remained in an abstracted state so that it took him by surprise when, before entering the cab he had hailed, she flung wide apart her arms, allowing her coat to fall open, and embraced him as if she meant to smuggle him away inside its furry warmth. He smelled the randy mix of perfumes from her hair, her face powder, her clothes. He was aware of every place his body touched hers—the large soft breasts, the drumhead of belly, the stanchion thickness of her thighs. And knew this was not his mother.

When he goes home, his mother will open the door to him. Mother, he will say, acknowledging not her presence but the inconceivability of her absence. She will pull him toward her proferred cheek as if directing the blind and he will give her the ritual kiss, a Zen-like kiss, empty of all intent, and he will enter, his hand still joined to hers, not knowing where one flesh ends, the other begins.

THE INHERITANCE

AT THE FUNERAL BOONE PLAYED HIS PART WITH DIGNIFIED restraint, concealing his disgust at that whole show of bereavement. His mother had died in bits and pieces, evicted room by room from her many-mansioned soul. She had paid little regard to the final demolition notice, nor would he, let Irene blubber all she would.

The only shock he felt was at the choice of service. He had expected burning, not a burial. Long ago his father had distributed two forms to the household with a clipped note: sign and return to me. Boone had read, signed, returned, thereby authorizing his cremation—no frills, please—and bequeathing to the needy all his organs like so many variety meats (still carried in his wallet the card advising whom it may concern of this prior lien on his body). Perhaps his mother had not signed. But how to explain the strict Lutheran service—an hour's worth of Lord Jesus Christ in chapel and an extra serving at the grave—if not by a sly recidivism on his mother's part? Not his father's, that was clear from the crotch-scratching, the muttering at graveside: "Then said I, Lord, how long?" Boone hoped only he had heard that groan. His own pose of painful attention was meant to serve as reprimand, he was not really listening to the familiar drone of earth to earth, ashes to ashes, dust to dust, eternal life through our Lord Jesus Christ, so that when the next words sprang out at him, de-ritualized, with all the ferocity of the literal, he felt skewered through the heart... *Who shall change our vile body, that it may be fashioned like unto His glorious body...* Boone gritted his teeth, not to cry out: Even a progressive degenerative disease? Vile body. In the genetic sweepstakes, his mother had drawn exactly that. His tears—the first and last he was to shed for her—were more of fury than of grief.

At the convivial aftermath of funeral meats, his father acting as bartender poured such stiff drinks that all those distant cousins (lapsed Lutherans too, Boone could only assume) dissolved more into hilarity than tears. Boone did not touch a drop, preferring sobriety to feed his disgust.

Let no one say his father lacked proper filial support. Since he no longer kept a car, Boone drove him to the monument yard to choose a stone. That is, provided the car—his father insisted on taking the wheel. I know the way, he offered as an excuse, as if he drove every day along that remote stretch of highway hysterical with flags of

used-car lots. Another form to fill out: the epitaph. The
charge made by letter count, his father turned laconic, put
down just her name, her dates. Boone thought some sen-
timent should be added. In verse. Such as:

> Now with our Lord Jesus Christ
> Who is a Whiz
> At changing such vile bodies
> Like unto His.

He played good brother too, moving Irene back home.
All those years of sublets were now explained: always a tiny
studio up five walk-up stairs, with an alcove for the daybed,
a closet for the kitchen, and a bath down the hall; always
the same thin Indian cotton bedspread, the same thread-
bare oriental on floors black with old varnish, each new
room suffering the same diseases of decrepitude, from the
psoriasis of flaking ceilings to the ascites of bulging walls.
What more did a body need when on the waiting list for
just this vacancy?

He did all the lugging while she stood on the brown-
stone stoop, warning him which cartons should be handled
with more care. Even in that bitter cold, she kept her
outerwear to hand-knitted shawls. Layering, she called it.
With cossack boots and ankle-length wool skirt, she had
a turn-of-the-century look, right out of steerage. "Don't
drop that one," she called out, hugging herself for warmth,
"it's got my elephants." She collected elephants, but only
elephants with trunks upraised—a good-luck symbol.
Unfortunately the trunks were always breaking off. He
controlled his temper, even stayed to clear away the stor-

age boxes cluttering her old room. His father hung about, carefully stepping out of the way; looking on, but never offering to lend a hand. You would think he was moving out, not Irene in. And after all her stuff was carried up the stairs, more boxes to be carried down. Leave those in the hall, Irene instructed, Good Will would pick them up tomorrow.

"Glad to see you're getting rid of stuff," he said with an obtuseness remembered ever after with a painful flush. "I've never known a house so full of junk."

"They're mother's things." Irene let that sink in. "Never mind, Boone, it's only right I should have that job."

My things. He heard his mother plain.

"There was a box—" he had to squeeze the words out through a bolus in his throat—"she kept it in the top drawer of her dresser. You didn't throw that out, by any chance?"

To hide whatever might show in his eyes, he glared at the cartons. Irene laughed: he looked like he was playing Superman again, using his x-ray vision. It would be easier if he just told her what kind of box.

"Red lacquer. One of those sleek shiny jobs. Like something in which a Japanese would pack his lunch."

Twelve, thirteen he must have been when he first looked at her and saw a middle-aged woman with a name other than mother. Mary Ashton Everready. Had she been pretty, Mary Ashton? It was a peculiar family, he knew by then, that kept no photographs. His father seemed to feel they were a mnemonic device for people of low intellect. "I keep it all right here," he'd say and tap his head. As for his

mother, "There are some people who are simply born
unphotogenic," she confessed, as to another congenital disease. Irene had told him that, before the days of plastic
surgery, they shot aging movie stars through cameras
screened with gauze; he tried for the same effect by looking through his lashes.

"Why are you squinting at me that way, Boone?"

"I was just wondering what you looked like before you
married Dad."

Mock amazement in that exaggerated lift of brow. But
she was pleased, he knew that from her eyes. The wry purs-
ing of her mouth warned him she was about to say something sharp, her way of discounting any complimentary
attention. "What you mean is—" but still she flushed—
"you can't believe I was ever young." With a laugh—at
him? at herself?—she opened the dresser drawer, burrowed
in a lot of filmy stuff, pulled out the box. "Mind, you're not
to ever touch my things," she warned.

A box of such high polish seemed fit repository for
state secrets. Out came a passport, its mottled green showing travel wear at the edges. Slipping off the rubber band
that held it to some envelopes with foreign stamps, she
made ready to show him that her youth had been officially
notarized. "Oh no!" she screeched and hid her face behind
fingers spread like a fan, "I never looked like that!" Back
snapped the band, back slid the passport, back went the box.

Of course the first time he found himself alone in the
house he sneaked a look. Almost his nerve failed him—the
crime not so much in laying hands on her private papers as
in putting his gross touch on the snake-like tangle of her

nylons, on the empty cups of her bras. His fingers left sweat marks on the lacquer, he had trouble lifting off the top. The envelopes banded to the passport were ancient, dated by the postmark, of a kind of flimsy paper he had never seen before. Addressed to Mary Ashton, not his mother. His mother, he corrected himself, before his mother was his mother. Love letters, they had to be—girls always kept them like hidden treasure. From his father, before his father was his father? Foreign stamps, but no return address; so his father was a traveler even then. He would have liked to know how such a man sounded when he spoke of love, but felt the full weight of that biblical injunction: no son should see his father naked. And if fear of God was not enough to stop him, fear of his mother was. Such thin paper was sure to crumble with the unfolding—a dead give-away. Still he took comfort in this evidence that they had loved each other—selfish comfort, sandwiching himself between their love, snuggling in it like a small child in his parents' bed. Nobly putting aside the letters, he opened the passport instead. Just as ancient, issued to a Mary Ashton too. Dry-throated, he drank in the forbidden view. A kind of terror squeezed his heart: the eyes of this young and pretty woman held no knowledge of his existence. She stared straight back and cut him dead.

"I know the box you mean," Irene said. "It had papers, personal stuff, I gave all that to Dad." She turned on him the forgiving look he so hated, its only purpose to make clear he had much to be forgiven for. "I had to go through everything, no one to help, I couldn't very well ask Dad, not in the state he's in. You know what I found hardest? Her underwear. What is there about underwear," she asked plaintively, "that's so painful when it belongs to someone dead?"

Boone was glad his was not the hand. Don't touch my things, he would have heard her cry.

He stood in the doorway watching his father pack his bag. A meticulous packer. As if every garment had a natural grain in accordance with which he made those precise folds with the edge of his palm. Even the knitted jockey shorts. Boone could feel the heat of anger like an alcoholic glow, even as he marveled at the smooth compression of a voluminous dark blue robe with satiny lapels—the kind never worn by any other mortal save Ronald Colman in movies of the thirties.

"So you've wangled another trip, I see. You haven't lost much time." The doorway in which he stood, the doorway to his parents' bedroom, was used to framing a more plangent cry. *There he goes again, off to some god-forsaken spot, bringing back god-knows-what diseases.* Even in her mobile days, his mother had not liked those survey trips abroad. She, for whom catastrophe was always hovering in the wings, was certain that it but awaited his father's departure to strike the plumbing, the children, or the car.

"I don't have much time." A half-moment of silence as absolute as zero. Was his father too about to die? "Next year they're retiring me, you know. After that—" he shrugged— "I dwindle into a part-time consultant."

Boone was unmoved. It was in the nature of fathers to dwindle. As a child he had watched his father pack as for an epic journey, seeing a Moses who crossed wildernesses to strike a rock with his staff: this is the site! And lo, Tower and Rowe would send forth its minions to construct the dam, needless to say gargantuan in size (something like the Grand Coulee was what he had in mind)—one of those mighty sweeps of concrete that looked like Niagaras of water turned to stone, whose main function (as he now saw it) was neither flood control nor the generation of electricity but, like the Great Pyramids it rivaled, the advertisement of its builder's power. To discover that minihydros were his father's specialty, what a come-down. As for those epic journeyings, they were finagled by his father, much as a congressman contrives a junket, whenever he craved a respite from the drudgery of computerized design, a holiday from office politics. From wife and children, too? his mother must have wondered.

Still, give the man credit—he had always returned. And it couldn't have been easy. Boone recalled his early dating years, how girls liked to break the ice with horror stories about their families. When his turn came, he found himself employing an engineer's vocabulary: tension, compression, stresses, trusses. Do you know how an arch works, he would ask, then quote his father quoting da Vinci: An arch consists of two weaknesses which leaning one against the other makes a strength.

He wanted to be fair, even generous, but the familiar sense of holiday exuded by the packing still enraged him. He watched his father lock the case, secure it further by buckling its two broad straps. No flight-weight, easy-to-carry nylon for a man who still wore dressing gowns. The worn leather, kept buttery soft with constant saddle-soaping, announced to all the world that here was a man who, forced to give his custom to the airlines, in his heart still rode the trains.

"I'm glad to see that you are not exactly paralyzed with grief."

"Is that what you want—a paralytic on your hands?"

"All I want is that red lacquer box of mother's. Irene says she gave it to you." A puzzled look was all his father gave him in answer. "I don't see that it's so unreasonable to want something of hers to keep for myself. Call it my inheritance, if you like."

"Of course, of course. I was just trying to remember where I put it. Probably in the closet—yes, I'm sure, on the top shelf. See if it's there."

It was. Boone tucked it under his arm and stalked out. And stalked back in.

"There's nothing in it, damn you!"

"It's the box you meant, isn't it?" That dawn of under-standing enacted in his father's face—pure pretense, Boone inwardly raged. "You don't mean you wanted those old love letters? Had I known—I never thought—she was so pri-vate, I'm surprised she told anything about it. Too bad, son, I threw them out, I'm afraid."

"There was a passport, with her picture. I suppose that's in the garbage too." Coldly he observed his father's grimace, a sudden crumpling of flesh like newsprint added to a fire just before it goes up in flame. Behold the poor widower in his grief? Even before he could re-use the sneer "pure pretense," his father's face had re-assumed its more familiar corrugated hardness. Like a store front iron-shuttered after closing, his mother had once muttered, preferring arguments to end in fire, not ice.

Boone remembered now to be surprised that there had ever been love letters between those two. "But I'm not surprised you junked them. You fought like cats and dogs, not what I would call a happy marriage. And then came all the doctor bills. You must be glad they're over, why pretend to mourn?"

"A happy marriage," his father repeated, a man bemused, bobbing his head thoughtfully. For a moment Boone mistook the ruminative gesture for his mother's nerve-damaged wobble, then almost laughed in relief. With laughter, as always, anger oozed away, a boil that had burst. In its stead, a tenderness, a warm flush of love coursing through his body like a transfusion of someone else's blood. Why are we always out of sync, he wondered sadly, not taken in by his father's smile, seeing below it the flat tautness of a cobra's neck.

"A happy marriage!" Appreciative repetition, as if Boone had turned a particularly felicitous phrase. "How could I have missed that one, it should head the list!"

Boone eyed him cautiously, asked what list.

"Don't tell me you've forgotten. Poor little rich girl? Wise fool? Honest thief?"

Boone remembered. With his father, it was always word games. He was now being instructed to add happy marriage to the family's list of oxymorons. Happy marriage: the ultimate contradiction in terms. "Come on, dad, you don't mean that, any more than I mean what I just said about you and mother not being happy—"

"Happy, happy, happy." Sarcasm had always been his father's mode of child abuse. Hit me, Boone silently pleaded, as he had when a child, but his father never would. "Lately, I notice, happiness has taken on the aspect of a constitutional right. Guaranteed by the founding fathers. Life, liberty and the pursuit of. A bit weasily, wouldn't you say, that wording. Typical of lawyers."

Boone waited. Was that all? His father folded and refolded a still damp towel as if that occupied all his thoughts. Boone edged toward the door, content to have offered a manly apology.

"Sit down, Boone. You've charged me with unhappiness—a cardinal sin. Allow me the courtesy of a defense."

Both chairs were occupied with piles of clothes. No place to sit but the bed. The long shelf above the headboard still demarcated his mother's from his father's side: hers the flat uneven stacks of paperback mysteries, green Penquins of the classic English school; his the upright hardbacks, thick-spined, mostly from university presses— a history buff's light reading. He chose his mother's side, hoping for less gore.

"You can use a short lecture on American history— what are you grinning at?"

Boone was adding "short lecture" to the oxymoron list. "Nothing, dad," he said, not without appreciation of his father's stance. What else but the full-hour lecturer's pose: one elbow resting on the highboy chest, fingers interlocked, a teepee formed with opposing thumbs. Like—the memory brought Boone perilously close to tears—his mother's game with baby hands: here is the church, here is the steeple . . .

"I'll keep in mind that you constructed models of the Nina, Pinta and Santa Maria in the third grade, thereby covering the subject to the satisfaction of the Board of Ed, but since you brought up that hallowed clause—"

Boone opened his mouth, closed it. Pointless denial.

"—let me ask you, do you not find it odd that those worthy squires, the original best-government-is-the-least-government crew, concerned themselves with a right—if you can call it that—so difficult to define and impossible to enforce? The pursuit of happiness!" Words his father rolled off his tongue as if mocking another idiocy of his son's coinage. "Now what do you think they meant by that? Since it's the one right you choose to exercise, I'm sure you've given some thought to what you're chasing."

Boone half rose, ready to admit to ignorance, to idiocy, anything, let him but leave the room.

"Before you commit yourself," the stern voice pressed him back, "let me remind you these were gentlemen of the Enlightenment, they knew their Latin, life required the sacrifice of private joys to civic virtue. As sensible men, their definition of happiness might strike you as overly modest. Something like—"

Into Boone's mind flashed a tee shirt with a Charlie Brown definition (or was it one of Snoopy's?) that he had treasured on his chest.

"—retirement in old age, a small estate somewhere in the country, no more public duties, time at last to observe nature and read Catullus."

Boone shook his head. Too long for a tee shirt.

"All right," his father said, accepting correction. "Some may have leaned toward the Benthamite persuasion—the greatest happiness of the greatest number—but were told to keep it down to 25 words or less. Needless to say, if you consult the courts, all they meant by that fine phrase was the right to get—and keep—your own. There you have it—man's highest aspirations reduced to tee shirt wisdom—" Boone raised startled eyes: had his father read his mind?—"happiness is: the private ownership of property. I've often thought it was their one mistake, that particular passage. Maybe this nation's history would have been different, truer to their original intent, had they only written: life, liberty and the pursuit of meaningful work. Most men would find that happiness enough. But you—you—" fingers stood out in a tetany of controlled anger and Boone mouthed *out come the people*, taking childish comfort in finishing the rhyme—"you would never settle for something as ephemeral as that, what you want is a really solid achievement—a glorious everlasting fuck!"

Don't let a lion lick you, Irene had once warned him (unnecessarily, it seemed at the time), its tongue will take your skin off. So will Dad's, Boone had scoffed.

"As for your mother and me—"

"Forget it, forget I mentioned mother, forget the whole thing," Boone pleaded and fled.

"For your information—" his father called down the hall—"those letters weren't from me!"

Boone stopped, did not turn around, neck muscles tensed, shoulders hunched, as if the flesh knew better than he the bombardment had not ceased.

"They're from her first love!" his father shouted, determined to be heard, however great the distance. "First and only love, need I say?"

Behind him, Boone heard a door slam. Down the stairs his feet, stumbling, led him. Into the kitchen, as if just home from school, as if his mother would be there, heating milk for his hot cocoa.

"You look like you could stand a pick-me-up," Irene said, hovering by the stove, waiting for the kettle to boil. He sat down heavily at the dark oak table (*no plastic in this house!* his mother's battle cry), willing to be administered to even by his sister.

"Sometimes it hits that way—as an aftershock," Irene said, placing before him a steaming cup.

He hardly heard her. Was vaguely aware there was something he should tell her. Or did she know already that the load-bearing element in this family structure was their father? He brushed his hand across his face, as if to cancel out all engineering terms, slow to realize the wetness was from tears. A man doesn't cry, his father had been taught, but had failed to pass the lesson on to him. Inhaling the vapor of some strange herbal brew, he thought: Here I am, in the house I grew up in, and I no longer know my way about.

PETS

THE BOX OF CHEESE CRACKERS PICTURED A SCHOOL OF
little golden fish (for so the crackers were shaped), all traveling from left to right with one exception. A swirling line
showed the wake of the sharp turn taken by the lone mav-
erick heading in the opposite direction. Unlike his blank-
faced peers, this piscine drop-out had a black dot for an
eye and a black upward curve for a smile.

Munching crackers by the handful, Amy would stare
back at the black dot until her politely closed mouth, con-
taining the crumbs, took on an upward curve of its own,
reflecting the little fish's smirk. He's cute, was all she
thought at first; she had munched her way through three
boxes (22 oz. each) before she realized what her favorite

was up to. All the other fish were swimming blindly into her maw, to be chomped and masticated and swallowed, but *that* little fish, not eyeless like the others, could see what was coming, had no intention of following the others to certain destruction. Starting with this contrary individualist on the box front, she counted twenty-one fish before she came to its duplicate on the box back. Another twenty-one before she returned to its image on the front. From that time on, she ate twenty-one fish, put one aside, ate another twenty-one, put one aside—a ritual not to be broken.

~~

What Amy needed was a pet. Although her father, Mark, and her mother, Toby, argued about who had suggested it first, they were in agreement that what was needed was a dog.

"I don't like dogs," Amy whined.

Toby cajoled her with visions of a fluffy puppy as amenable to affection as a stuffed toy. Mark ignored her to show his disapproval of whining. A dog was just the thing, they assured each other, just as once they had assured each other a baby was just the thing. The baby, as if aware the matter was of some urgency, had been a "preemie."

They would never feel so close again as when they donned white masks to behold for the first time the tiny creature protected from them by a plastic tent. Gazing down on a idea jointly conceived and carried to completion, or as near as made no difference, they groped for each other's hand. Mark said, "She looks like you," although secretly he thought she had a way to go before she looked like anything. Toby said, "Oh no, she looks like you."

"I'd rather have a cat," Amy said, without much hope.

"You don't know what you want," Toby said and reminded her about the fish. What do you want for your birthday, they had asked. A goldfish in a bowl, she had said. All that trouble and expense—a 30-gallon tank, aerators, filters, heater, thermostat, lighting, the best gravel to support a balanced seafloor of aquatic plants, and two magnificent specimens of that exotic member of the goldfish family, the oranda, each six inches long and guaranteed to keep growing.

"Ooh" and "aah" was the general response of viewers to the lavish fins and double-lobed tail trailing through the water like golden veils. "Ugh" was the appalled reaction of the few who found the over-sized head with fleshy overgrowths too like the monstrous deformities of the Elephant Man. "They are very easy to keep, they eat anything," Mark and Toby would inform their awestruck guests, modestly downplaying the product of centuries of genetic manipulation they had purchased. But Amy never gave them a glance.

"Let's get to the point," Mark said, overriding female squabbling with firm masculine logic. "Fish aren't pets." A cat? He moved his hand like a teetering balance—a cat didn't quite make the grade. But a dog, he promised his daughter, she would see, a dog was something else. A dog would be someone to come home to, someone always waiting at the door (Ah, that must be your father, his mother would say, recognizing the car's peculiar knock halfway up the block), someone thrown into a paroxysm of anxiety should they be delayed beyond the usual hour of their return (What can be keeping him? his mother would ask, keeping vigil at the window for a glimpse of headlights in the early evening gloom).

Yes, Toby said, a dog made sense. (In her youth there had been a golden retriever who had met the ultimate test for devotion: killed while running across the street to greet her.)

"I'd rather have a cat," Amy said, without hope.

~~

Amy's grandmother, breeder of champions, was not so sure about the dog. Particularly when Toby asked for one from her kennel. Afghans, she warned her daughter over the telephone, did not have the sycophantic make-up that children required of pets. Nor had Amy, on her annual visits, shown any interest in the dogs.

"It will be different when she has one of her own," Toby said.

That has a familiar ring, Mrs. Russell refrained from saying. Asked instead how were things, meaning Mark. "Fine," her daughter snapped, thereby confirming her suspicion that things were not. Adding a newcomer to the menage had been tried before; it hadn't worked then, it wouldn't work now. Speaking from personal experience—though Mrs. Russell knew better than to speak at all—she had found it far easier to arrange an amicable divorce than an amicable marriage.

Ha, Toby thought, reading her mother's silence correctly. No way I'm going to end up like her, with a Christmas card list studded with ex-husbands. "So what about the dog?" she prodded. Silence made audible in a sigh. "We're not asking for a future champion, just the one in Sheba's litter that doesn't quite come up to your high standards," and added to herself: the one that otherwise you'd put down.

A deeper sigh. Mrs. Russell wished she had not mentioned Sheba's new litter. Quickly she calculated when school let out. Six weeks before Amy would make her usual visit. The pups would be weaned by then, old enough to display any flaws. "We'll see," she said—that time-honored formula for giving in.

In the mirror over the phone, a face that could pass for that of a durable high-fashion model. Thank God, Mrs. Russell thought, for good bones. Then, turning self-critical, rebuked the beauty in the mirror: you're just too generous for your own good.

~~

"What are these crackers doing in your sock drawer?" Toby asked, looking her disgust. "You know you're not to leave food in your room, it'll bring roaches, I've told you that."

Amy let out a screech. Like a cat whose tail has been stepped on, Toby told her she sounded, and disposed of the cache over the wastebasket in a shower of crumbs. Stale as the crackers were, had they been left whole she wouldn't put it past Amy to dig them out and eat them. Amy would eat anything, and showed it.

"Don't look like that," Toby commanded and resumed her packing. "There are supermarkets where you're going. Your grandmother won't starve you." The child looked unconvinced. Toby tried to turn her thoughts away from food. "And just think, when you come back, you'll have a little puppy all your own." Still that sullen look. And that slow-motion dressing when they had hardly time to catch the plane. "Must you wear white tights with that short skirt?" she snapped. "They only make your thighs look fatter."

In the taxi more talk about a puppy, but Amy did not listen. She was reading. She read with a deconstructionist's eye: a text was a text was a text. *Passenger must use curb side to disembark. No eating or drinking in cab. Passengers must pay all bridge and tunnel tolls. Driver not required to change bills larger than $20.00. Please sit back in case of short stop. Thank you for not smoking.* She preferred the subway to a cab—the reading material was not so quickly exhausted. And more of a challenge, so many of the advertisements being in Spanish. The pictures helped. And often there were side-by-side English versions.

With nothing more to read, Amy began to count the highway overpasses they drove under. They were all fenced now to protect against the dropping of cement blocks on car roofs, the hurling of rocks against windshields. There were different designs, she noticed: some high fences, some a single heavy strand of wire making tall loops in close array, like the first exercise she had been given for cursive writing.

Toby, giving up on her, tried talking to the driver. Not very easy through bullet-proof glass and besides he didn't understand much English. Amy read his identification card hanging from the front dashboard. His name looked French but he was the wrong color. "Are you from Haiti?" Toby directed through the little hole for passing money, and at his nod began practicing her French. Amy hated French, hated her teacher who was always picking on her pronunciation, but who had complimented her on Toby's. Amy could see them rattling away at each other at the parents conference, talking through their noses about where to eat and shop in Paris. At least that was all that Toby had reported back to Mark over dinner. Amy doubted there had been time to get around to her. Spanish would be *her* language, Amy decided. The best thing about it was that she didn't need a teacher. Abortion, crime prevention, Aids, alcohol abuse, food stamps were words she already knew. And she could say this coffee had that down-home flavor, these cigarettes have real taste.

At the airport, Toby attacked her again with little attentions, adjusting her backpack, presenting her with an unopened pack of gum, reminding the woman at the check-in counter that the stewardess should be alerted that this little girl was traveling alone. That was embarrassing. "I've been making this trip since I was five," Amy informed the clerk. "Alone?" the woman asked. "All alone," Amy said, and was rewarded by the look of wonderment on the woman's face.

By the time they reached the gate, Amy sensed that Toby had already left her. Which was just as well. She went through the metal-detector with the confidence of one carrying no weapon and turned to wave the expected goodbye. Toby waved back but with such an abstracted gaze, Amy was not sure at whom. When she entered the plane, a stewardess took her in tow. She could have found her seat herself. And she didn't want her backpack in the bin overhead, she wanted it under her feet. "I know how," she said and grabbed the buckle out of the stewardess' hand. "My, you're quite a big girl, aren't you?" the stewardess said, no longer cooing. Fat was what she meant, Amy knew, and stuck her tongue out at the receding back. From the pocket in the seat ahead, she drew out the diagrammed instructions for jettisoning over water and began to read.

~~

On these annual summer visits, Mrs. Russell had come to accept her granddaughter much as she did the dogs she boarded: the child was taken in with the same responsible commitment, provided the right food for growing bones, plenty of yard exercise and (though this was an extra the dog-owners paid dearly for) firm but gentle training sessions to render her a more agreeable companion indoors. If this time Mrs. Russell expected of Amy a more intimate relationship, it was not with herself but with the dogs. She turned off the TV to ask, "Wouldn't you like to go down to the kennels with me?"

Amy said neither yes nor no, but hoisted herself up (prone on the floor was her favorite position). *Wouldn't you like?* she had learned by now, was a mere politeness prefixed to a command. She carefully closed the package of goldfish, holding the top edges together, folding them over twice and bending in the little flaps on each side, buttoned the flap of her shirt pocket to keep safe her new cache of "pets" salvaged from destruction, then followed her grandmother out of the house. There was a long slope of lawn to be crossed before they reached the two brick kennels with their fenced-in runs. The grass was thick and closely cropped. It looked especially designed to lie on and look up at white clouds changing shape. Or at least to walk on bare-footed, feeling the tickle of its nap between the toes. But "we can't have that," her grandmother had said. Ticks, she had warned, Lyme disease.

A hysterical noise from one of the kennels greeted their approach. That one was occupied by the "boarders," to be bypassed for the other, reserved for Mrs. Russell's champions. The Afghans were outside in their run, two putting it to good use by galloping at full speed its full length, then turning on a dime to race back. Another was reclining supine on a low wooden platform, hind legs spread open, like a sunbather determined to tan all over. A she, even Amy could tell, from the embarrassing display of swollen tits. "That's your puppy's mother," Mrs. Russell pointed out, "she feels a little put out because we are weaning her litter." Beneath the trouserings of hair, the sex of the other two was concealed. Dog-walkers in the park, Amy had noticed, had no shame; if necessary, they would bend over to see what was there, but Amy thought that rude.

The bitch had merely turned her head, leaving it to loll in their direction, but these two loped up to the fence to greet them with a haughty stare. Just because they were champions didn't mean they had to be so snooty, Amy objected. "You have a lot to learn about Afghans," was Mrs. Russell's impatient reply. "They're near-sighted, you see, and when they get up close, they have to hold their heads back to get a clear image." But Amy had turned her back on the explanation to stare at the other kennel where a man in overalls was hosing down the concrete run. The boarders, penned inside, kept up the barking, whining, yapping, baying. To Amy it sounded like a horde of ravening beasts, straining on their leashes, clawing at the doors. In response, she clutched at the sturdy twill of her grandmother's divided skirt.

"You're not afraid of dogs, are you?" Mrs. Russell asked. Amy heard in her tone the demand for an immediate denial. "Not exactly" she temporized. "Are they mad because they're locked up?" Mrs. Russell corrected her firmly. Amy mustn't assume a dog was mad just because it barked. The boarders were an anxious lot, they got excited when they heard anyone outside. After all, it could be their family coming to take them home.

From the stubborn set of the child's face, it was clear that she held to her original opinion. Mrs. Russell gave the deep sigh of patience sorely tried. Could not decide who tried her patience more—that retarded son of a local farmer she had just hired or her own grandchild. Reminded that, if left on his own, Lucas would play with the hose all day, she called him over. He had a funny kind of walk, Amy noticed—feet splayed way out, arms loosely dangling from his trunk. He greeted her with a half-smile and a "Hi, kid." The half-smile was still there when Mrs. Russell spoke to him sharply. Amy decided he was very good-natured.

"That's enough," Mrs. Russell said. "As soon as it dries a bit, let the dogs out. And after lunch, you'd better mow the paddock. I want that grass kept nice and short."

Speaking of lunch, she said, the puppies. Amy, well-trained to keep at heel, followed her inside the kennel.

Awakened from their sleep, the future champions bounded toward them, bigger than puppies had any right to be, to Amy's way of thinking. They encircled Mrs. Russell, shouldering each other to get closer, shouldering Amy away too, just another obstacle.

"Ah, you're hungry, my pretties," Mrs. Russell said, "that's good." Amy wondered at such approval just for wanting food. She was hungry all the time but no one said, "that's good."

The kennel had its own kitchen, of which Mrs. Russell was justly proud—so well-designed it had twice been featured in the American Breeders journal. At the long high counter (out of reach of greedy feeders), she began preparing the midday meal, with a running commentary for Amy's benefit. Like a cooking show on TV, Amy thought. Amy liked cooking shows. To her they were a magic act, with all that chop-chop, whisk-whisk, stir-stir, lacking nothing but a drum roll at that final moment of high drama when the oven door was opened and out came the finished dish.

" . . . now we add the grated vegetables to the meat, break in this slice of whole wheat toast. A little bone flour stirred into the gravy and we mix it all up, like this, and there we are."

All mushed up together—yuk, went Amy's stomach. She hated one food even touching another. What she liked best about TV dinners were the neat partitions in the foil tray. Next best was eating in a restaurant, where she always ordered mashed potatoes. With them you could construct a series of dams, keeping the gravy away from the peas, the peas away from the carrots, the carrots away from the meat. Stop playing with your food, Mark would order, but she wasn't playing, she was repairing leaks.

"Now you take this one to your own puppy," Mrs. Russell said, thrusting a bowl into her hands.

But which was her puppy? They all looked alike.

The one with the cow hocks, Mrs. Russell almost snapped, exasperated by such an undiscriminating eye. Stopped herself just in time. "This one," she said, patting a silky topknot. Made sure not to weight her words with judgment. "If you look closely, you will see that his hind feet turn out a little."

Amy looked. Made that hiccoughing sound which was her rendition of laughter. It rasped against Mrs. Russell's nerves. So did the stubby-fingered hand plastered against the mouth, as if to prevent the spread of germs.

"I know what," Amy spluttered, "I'll call him Lucas."

A peasant's hand, Mrs. Russell thought with an inward shudder. And wondered again if she had done right not to put the puppy down.

The noise of the mower distracted them both. Mrs. Russell dismissed it—that Lucas, like a child with a toy, couldn't even wait until after lunch—but Amy ran to the door.

"It's like a real tractor!" she cried. "With a steering wheel and everything!"

Two of a kind, Mrs. Russell muttered, but did not call her back when she dashed outside. Yes, yes, all right, she said quickly when Amy dashed back in to excitedly announce, "Lucas says he can show me how, Lucas says it's easy as pie!"

First between Lucas's spread knees, then all by herself, Amy drove the tractor-mower over the lawn, around the paddock, back over the lawn, even down to the meadow already cropped by a first haying. Every day Amy drove, with a look of wild exhilaration that made Mrs. Russell think of a pilot at high altitude, oxygen-deprived. "Wouldn't you like—?" Mrs. Russell politely commanded. "No, thank you," Amy politely returned the serve and mounted the mower. Conceding defeat, Mrs. Russell instructed Lucas to make sure the blades were lifted lest all her acreage be mowed completely bald. Noticed that this usurpation of his favorite machine had left Lucas as sulky as Sheba. "Never mind, Lucas, she'll be leaving the end of next week," she reassured them both. And aside from a severe warning about rabies, in case she ran into any raccoons, Amy was left on her own.

This time at the airport it was the puppy who got the special attention. Amy was left in the waiting area while Mrs. Russell went off to see that Sirhan was properly cared for in flight. (Lucas was a very fine name, her grandmother had tactfully apologized, but the offspring of a champion were registered by name at birth.) She took notice that nothing was said at the check-in counter about her traveling alone. Feeding her resentment with goldfish, she watched the exuberant play of three little girls, the tallest her own age, she judged. All three had thick shiny hair that bounced as they ran and eyes bright as new pennies. They were dressed funny—no one dressed like that at school—

in wide flouncy skirts with sashes that tied in the back, white socks and shiny black shoes. When they leaned over to pull up their socks, you could see their underpants.

The real point of the game, she soon figured out, was sliding in patent leather shoes on the marbleized floor. It looked like fun—next time, she decided, she wouldn't wear sneakers. The youngest fell, ran crying to the large woman with the baby seated next to Amy. There, there, the mother said absently, busy with nursing. " She's not hurt," Amy assured her, "she fell on her behind."

The child lifted her face from the mother's lap to stare at the deliverer of so obtuse an observation. The tears continued to flow, but silently, like a tap left on absentmindedly, while this stranger was surveyed. The gaze became fixed on the crackers. "Want some?" Amy asked, and needing no answer, began to place them one by one into the open palm. With virtuoso slides, the other two suddenly drew up beside her. It was like feeding pigeons, Amy thought and resigned herself to a severe depletion of her stock. One by one, into the extended palms. Not that she was doling them out, but she had to keep strict count.

Boarding had just been announced when Mrs. Russell returned. "Those are my friends," Amy said, pointing out the girls now hovering around their mother.

"Pretty children," Mrs. Russell acknowledged, "Maybe you will be seated near them."

"That's their mother," Amy said, "I watched her feed the baby from her breast. It was very interesting."

Mrs. Russell looked her disgust at such a ludicrous figure. Big breasts pushing forward, enormous rump extending far back. You get something like that at times with the mismating of two incompatible breeds. Responding to the stare, the woman turned her head. Mrs. Russell looked away but not before the hard judgment: what in her dogs she would call a dish face. She looked again at the little girls—she had not been mistaken, they were lovely. Even the baby, thrown over the shoulder like a sack of grain, smiling at all the strangers, was charming. Where did it come from? With dogs you knew.

She gave her granddaughter a convulsive hug—a guilty hug that said "poor thing." Stayed to watch that receding form, ungainly enough without the added hump of a back-pack, disappear down the long corridor. Then, before start-ing on the long drive back, refreshed herself in the ladies' room. Checked her makeup in the mirror. Where does it come from, she asked that beauty. Who shrugged, glad to be going home to her dogs.

~~

Where was the camcorder? When was the last time they used it? Toby accused Mark of consumerism—buying every new gadget and then losing interest. Mark accused Toby of obsessive tidiness—putting everything away where no one could find it. "I know where it is," Amy said, and dug it out of the front hall closet, hidden by the winter coats and umbrellas. It had been put away in the original packing box, along with the tapes they had made when both it and Amy were new acquisitions. The tapes were labeled Baby at One; Baby at Two; Baby at Three.

"Baby?" Amy asked. "Is that me?"

"Of course, Baby as in Baby's Book, like the one

mother kept on me," Toby said. "A sign of the times—instead of a book, a miniseries for TV."

Removing the camcorder from its packing, Mark was as excited as if it were new. "Can you believe it?" he cried. "I had completely forgotten we had this thing."

Amy was excited too. "Are we going to make more TV movies of me?" she asked. "Can I wear makeup now? Everyone wears makeup for TV, even the men."

"We'll see," Toby said absently, giving Sirhan a good brush.

With the camcorder resting on Mark's shoulder (this neanderthal model weighs a ton, he complained), Toby went out to ring the doorbell so that Sirhan could be shot loping to the door, reacting to her entrance in a frenzy of joy, leaping up to lick her face. Then Toby took over the shooting and Mark rang the bell and Sirhan went through his act again. "Now you," Toby said, but Amy said she'd rather not. Who wanted to co-star with a dog?

While they were shooting Sirhan in the kitchen dogging Toby's footsteps as she prepared his meal, and Sirhan in the bedroom refusing to get off the bed, and Sirhan in the closet gnawing on one of Amy's old sneakers, Amy played those early tapes.

BABY AT ONE. Pale and puffy, a triumph of force-feeding, presiding over first birthday party. White-frosted cake is placed on high-chair tray. Toby leans over to blow out the one pink candle. Baby slips down until face is level with cake. Toby hoists up beanbag body with force of Heimlich maneuver. Doughy face falls into frosted cake. Toby laughs, suddenly sobers. Reams out frothy mouth with index finger. "Stop that damn thing," she shouts at Mark, still shooting away. "I think she's swallowed the candle!"

BABY AT Two. In the park, on a swing. This time it is Mark behind her, pushing so gently (any harder and she screams) the movement seems more that of the camera, as wielded by Toby's amateurish hand. "Zoom in," Mark directs and Toby zooms in. The moon face with its blond nimbus of wispy hair pulses like a planetary object, now approaching, growing fuller, features skewed and flattened by distortion, then receding into sharper focus, a round white object on whose surface are clearly visible a few indentations and small areas in relief—a landscape of desolation.

BABY AT THREE. On the beach, playing with a little friend. Both are clad in ruffled bikinis, complete with ruffled bras. Someone out of view is tossing them a beach ball, a gentle lob aimed to fall into the hoop of outstretched arms. With a timely squeeze, the friend holds her catch chest-high, screeching with delight. Much coaxing from the sidelines to persuade her to throw it back. Baby soberly awaits her turn, the ball is tossed, too late she brings her arms together. She looks amazed to find she is hugging nothing but herself.

Behind her Mark and Toby clapped—dutiful applause to signal end of lead-in, impatience for main event. Mark stepped around her prone form, reached for the eject button, new tape in hand.

"I want to run them over again," Amy whined.

"I remember now why we packed them away, you kept playing them over and over and each time you'd jump and down and cry that's me! that's me!" Mark said, inserted the new tape and pressed Play.

Amy humped herself up, got to her feet. "I'm ten now, I'm not a baby any more," she said.

Look at him, just look at him, Toby cooed, proudly smiling at the image on TV. All Amy could see was Sirhan looking straight at *them* and with the greatest disdain. "Let me know when I can watch The Avengers," she said and left them to it, trying hard for the haughtiness of the dog on the screen.

~~

The dog didn't work. Not that Toby admitted as much, but when her daughter called, Mrs. Russell could hear between the words.

"Everything's fine," was the first thing Toby said. Amy was back in school, Mark was working hard, staying so late she hardly ever saw him, she was working hard too. "But no more overtime, I'm firm about that. Sirhan expects me back at six and I don't like to keep him waiting for his walk."

Couldn't Amy walk him, Mrs. Russell asked, not concealing her disapproval. After all, it was Amy's dog.

Toby laughed—a warm clotted sound deep in her throat. "Tell that to Sirhan," she said. "He lets her put on the leash, then drags her to me. Even Mark has trouble with him. I'm the only one he obeys. Marks says it's a sex thing, I think he's actually jealous."

Afghans were like that, Mrs. Russell said noncommittally, they fix on one person.

"Anyway," Toby concluded, "we've decided to take a week off and go away—just the two of us. A kind of second honeymoon."

As bad as all that? Mrs. Russell wondered.

Amy, expecting the worst, was relieved to hear it was just a vacation. And that Edna, her old baby-sitter, would take over—she was used to Edna.

"Of course you are not a baby any more," Mark said so seriously that Amy knew it was a joke. "She'll be more of a house-sitter now."

"Dog-sitter, too," Toby added in that special voice she used for Sirhan, who loped to her side as if he knew he was the only dog around.

When Edna arrived, Mark and Toby were still arguing in their bedroom about the luggage—Mark shouting there was too much. "Hope he don't say that about me," Edna whispered to Amy, and held up a plastic shopping bag crammed with what she called her "things." Acting like a hostess, Amy took her to the guest room, pointed out which drawers of the chest were empty, and that the mattress on the daybed was new. Mark liked a hard one, she said, explaining more than she knew.

She wanted to watch Edna unpack, but Edna shooed her out. "Your folks are leaving, you'd better say goodbye," she said but Amy guessed she didn't want anyone to see her things. Which struck Amy as funny, since the things were always the same: pants, always navy blue, and tee shirts, always white. Toby had once given her a dark green one, with a crocodile on the pocket, for which Edna had said "thank you," but to Amy had confessed she needed white close to her face on account of the color of her skin. Amy liked her color, particularly on the high round forehead, without a furrow, which had the polished shine of their mahogany dining table.

Once the flurry of departure was over—the distracted hugs and kisses, the instructions about Sirhan, prominently posted in the kitchen but repeated orally—the house settled itself into the companionable peace controlled by a TV remote.

Edna was a martinet, strong on discipline, but Amy liked the way she governed—not by complaining but by strict rules. Toby would say: Must you eat a whole box of crackers right before dinner, no wonder at the table you just pick at your food. Edna said nothing about the crackers. Amy could play with her food as long as she liked but the last one at the table did the washing up. And white tights, Edna agreed, were high fashion, though the devil to get clean (she said nothing about fat thighs). No skin off her back, she shrugged, since she considered them as underwear. Which, according to the rules, Amy washed every night by hand.

As for Sirhan, Edna said she would fix his meals, but Amy was to do the walking. "But he doesn't like me" Amy whined. "He don't like me neither," Edna said, "we're not talking about like, we're talking about duty."

Amy resigned herself to duty. She would jiggle the leash, Sirhan would barely lift his head, then return to his despondent sprawl. She had to walk over, fix the hook to his collar and pull with all her strength. When tired of being dragged on his butt, he would get listlessly to his feet and allow her to lead him into the elevator and out of the building.

That was the weekend. Not so bad. The walks even provided a break in boredom. But Monday came, she returned from school, and routine resumed its sway. She threw down her book bag, opened a box of goldfish and sprawled in front of the TV.

"Duty first," Edna reminded her.

Shit and fuck, Amy said, but under her breath. (Foul language is one thing I won't stand for, Edna said.) Dutifully she took the leash and dragged Sirhan out, first stowing an emergency supply of crackers in her pocket. It was a sunny afternoon, more like July than September, and everyone was out—young couples, old ladies, babies, dogs and those scary people Mark called bums. Carefully Amy crossed the wide street to the park, walked along its stone retaining wall to the nearest entrance. Two new signs had been posted, Spanish on the right, English on the left, and a picture of a rat with skull and crossbones for the bilingually illiterate. She stole a glance at the English and then read: *Este Lugar contiene Veneno de Rata. Por favor, mantengan los perros atados y.* She was impressed with her fluency in Spanish, she knew exactly (more or less) what it said. And had two new words in her vocabulary. *Veneno:* poison. *Perros:* dogs. To fix them in memory, she repeated *Veneno:* poison, *Perros:* dogs. The two words put together had the iron ring of fate.

She looked at Sirhan. Dogs can't talk, she reassured herself, and began to plan what she would say. (I took him to that fenced-in dog run where you said he could be let off the leash, then someone came in with another dog and Sirhan ran out through the open gate, I'm sorry he found that poison, I'm sorry he's dead.) She leaned over and unhooked the leash. Stupid dog, just standing there. She gave him a little nudge with her foot. He turned his head, looked down his nose at her. "There in the grass!" she yelled. "See those little pellets? You're supposed to eat them!" Those inscrutable eyes were still fixed on her. Eat them yourself, they seemed to say.

Stupid dog, Amy muttered in defeat, reached out to releash him. Only then realizing he was free, the dog took off, covering the ground with his long graceful lope. Stop! Stay! Amy shouted and furious at being disobeyed gave chase, tantalized by his stop and go tactics—waiting until she neared him, then tearing off again. Hot and tired and out of breath, she came to her senses. If he got lost, wasn't that even better? And she could use the same story: the fenced-in dog run, Sirhan darting out, only leave out the bit about the poison.

Slowly she moved away, choosing a winding path edged by bushes which soon concealed her. Then sprinted for a farther exit, dawdled on the long walk back home to make it look like she had spent a lot of time trying to find him. Swinging the leash, she felt as freed on her end as Sirhan had felt on his. Still she made sure her face was crumpled with dismay when she rang the bell for Edna to let her in.

As soon as the door opened, she began: "I took him to that fenced-in run—" but Edna shut her up impatiently.

"Come in, come in, your mother's on the phone. Never mind the dog, he got here before you. The doorman found him waiting by the elevator, and I went down to fetch him."

Amy sent a poisonous look at the dejected form hunkered down on its floor bed, followed Edna to the phone. "Yes, she just came in," Edna was saying. "No, everything's all right. Yes, that's one smart dog all right . . . Sure, just like you got it down on the diet sheet, but he hardly eats a thing . . . I try, I try, but he just plain misses you..."

Amy jiggled from foot to foot, impatient for her turn. Pulled on Edna's shirt. They were still talking about Sirhan. At last Edna said, "Here she is," and handed her the phone.

"Hi," Amy said, and added for further identification, "it's me."

"Don't you ever, *ever*, let that dog loose again," was Toby's reply.

"I took him to the fenced-in dog run where you said—" Amy began, only to be interrupted again with the stern injunction never never to let Sirhan off the leash, no matter where; he would just have to wait for Toby's return for proper exercise. Which had better be soon or, from what Edna told her, he'd become skin and bones, the poor darling.

Tears of indignation welled in Amy's eyes. No one would listen to her perfectly legitimate excuse. She dug into her pocket, crammed her mouth with goldfish. "Are you having fun?" she managed to ask.

"Yes," Toby said. "Daddy's out fishing. He sends his love."

"I love him too," Amy spluttered.

"And I love you," Toby said formulaically then spoke her mind. "There's nothing wrong with *your* appetite, I can hear that quite clearly. *Must* you have your mouth full even when you're talking on the phone?"

Toby hung up. Yes I must, I must, I must, Amy silently jeered at the dead phone. Then thought: what a funny word must is. Must. Must. Must. Slowly masticating, she made a remarkable discovery. Words could be entirely divorced from meaning.

SERVANTS

HOWEVER REMARKABLY THAT HISTORIC MORNING DE-
veloped, it started out like any other, the daily catastrophe
striking a bit early perhaps—to be precise, at 8:45 a.m. A
strange male voice on the telephone (Eunice's brother, he
claimed) letting me know that their poor old mother had
had a stroke and Eunice would not be able to show up for
work that day. Or any day in the foreseeable future.

Not that I believed in the stroke. Or in the mother. Or
the brother. I counted up the score: Eunice was the fifth
to go in less than two years, making it three A.W.O.L.'s and
two dishonorable discharges, as Richard puts it. Although
he is a civilian, his procurement work with the Defense
Department has colored his vocabulary. He looks at me the

way I look at someone with three or four divorces in as many years: there must be something wrong with *me*.

And so there is, I suppose. I have never been comfortable with the concept of servants, not having been bred to it, and it is indicative of my discomfort that I never know what to call the women I hire. Servant, of course, has never been an acceptable word in America, as Mrs. Trollope noted even in the 1830's. Cleaning woman? But she spends half her time looking after my two- and four-year-old. Nanny? Too pretentious—and far too expensive. Housekeeper? I keep my own house, thank you. I fall back again on Mrs. Trollope's snide observations on American customs and call them "help." A cri de coeur.

Not for the first time, I thought of life before children—B.C., we dated all nostalgic references to those halcyon days—when I worked in a real office and not in our bedroom and the household chores were neatly divided, obviating the need for any hired assistance. How naive we were to think that the children would make no difference, not even to our income. I would be free-lancing at home, fully equipped with computer and modem and fax, fitting in the laundry and cleaning and cooking in my spare time, with the children always under my watchful eye, never entrusted to the care of strangers. Spare time—ah, there's the rub. Once I was immured in the house, Richard reverted to type, shedding all household responsibilities: he was the hunter, emerging from the cave every morning in search of wild game, and I his bedraggled mate whose function was to tend the fire, suckle the babes, prepare the food and anoint his wounds when he returned from his dangerous quest. As for my free-lance work for a book-packaging firm, surely that could be fitted in, much as our cave-dwelling forebears had found time to decorate their walls with all those paintings.

I am not a slow learner; before Robert was three months old, I was desperately calling employment agencies for part-time help. Two years later, pregnant with Sally, I settled for nothing less than full-time. Not difficult to find, if you paid enough, but difficult—at least for me—to keep.

It was a problem I no longer discussed with Richard. His liberal sympathies, with which I had heretofore agreed, required him to always side with the worker, a descriptive term never applied to me. When I fired our first one, I made the mistake of justifying myself: for all the hours she put in, I complained, the house was still filthy. The house looked as clean as it ever had, Richard responded with a shrug that made the reference pretty clear. I never said I cleaned well, I retorted, I hate housework. No doubt *they* hate housework too, he pointed out, it was not exactly the kind of job one could put one's heart and soul into. And what about *my* heart and soul, I wanted to scream, but once Richard started referring to them as *they*, I knew he had in mind the varying hues of black and brown that tinted our help—a kind of affirmative action that effectively took me out of competition with them in suffering. And, of course, bypassed the salient point Mrs. Trollope had made more than a hundred and fifty years before: that there was a peculiarly American horror of domestic service that rose above race and made incompetent servants of us all.

There was clearly no point in continuing the discussion. (The other time I fired one—"letting her go," I called it—I made no attempt to explain. I couldn't fault her cleaning, but she was so sullen and hostile that I kept raising her wages until I could no longer afford her.) As for Eunice's sudden departure from the scene, I hoped that Richard would believe in her mother's stroke more than I did and not chalk up another A.W.O.L. to my account.

Not that I had time to give to such a niggardly concern. It being a Monday, all the mess we had "saved" for Eunice over the weekend was now mine to dispose of. After dropping Robert off at nursery school, I put two loads of wash through the machine, vacuumed, made the beds, called the employment agency, managing between chores to rescue Sally from electrocution, decapitation, concussion and garbage-bag suffocation. Time to put her down for a nap. Tantrum. Screaming in my arms, she arched her back in what could have passed for the death throes of a victim of some strange South American arrow poison, grabbed the TV remote from a table as I carried her from the living room and hurled it against the TV screen.

Just as I dumped her in the crib, the doorbell rang. The exterminator, I figured. It was his day of the week.

Close, but no cigar. "Oh, it's you," I greeted my mother-in-law.

"It seems I've picked a bad time," she said, sweeping into the room. I use that word advisedly: she is a tall woman who favors long full skirts and voluminous capes and leaves a swirling mark through space as she moves. Also a wake of broken objets d'art, should any be exposed on low tables.

Fortunately, with two small children, we kept our tables pretty bare. She listened to my tale of woe—as much as she could hear over Sally's screams—with nothing but sympathy etched in her face and wondered vaguely if she could help. A polite offer, meriting a polite refusal, as we both knew, but I was beyond politeness.

"How sweet of you," I cooed, "if you could only take Sally for a little walk—the fresh air will quiet her down and give me a chance to catch my breath." She hesitated; it took only a little flattery to push her over the edge. "It's amazing how well you manage her—I wish you would tell me your secret."

You do catch more flies with honey—I wish I could remember that in dealing with Richard. She helped me stuff her struggling grandchild in the stroller and I pushed them both into the elevator, tracking their descent by the gradual distancing of the screams. From my window I watched her cross the street toward the park, stop and unzip Sally's jacket. Either it was warmer than I had thought or she was checking for signs of child abuse. Not caring which, I staggered to the living room couch, still littered with Sunday's papers, and collapsed on the Arts and Leisure section.

With only an hour before I had to pick up Robert, I knew I should get to work on the faxed copy waiting for me to edit. And check if there was anything in the freezer I could use for dinner. Unwilling to move, I took note that, although the bedrooms had been neatened, this room was still a mess. And so was my hair, itching for a shampoo. Instead of doing any of the above, I dug out the remote from under an armchair, resettled myself in the proper supine position and switched on the TV, confident of finding a movie on one or another channel—preferably an old black-and-white classic in which the hero was identifiable as such, the heroine kept her clothes on, and crime did not pay. I had an unbreakable rule not to watch TV during daylight hours (Sesame Street excepted) but a day like this—and only half over—was reason enough to break any unbreakable rule.

I was so exhausted I was content to stare at a blank screen for a full minute before I realized there was nothing to see. Damn that kid, she had broken the remote. Groaning at the exertion required for manual operation, I got to my feet but as I approached the TV I noticed the green light signifying that the set had been turned on. If not the remote, then the TV itself must have been damaged—a frustrating conclusion I refused to accept. I pushed every control on the panel—nothing happened. Proving that I could throw a tantrum too, I banged my fist against the top of the set and cursed the darkness. The picture came on.

What I saw was a man sitting with his back to the camera, confronting an elaborate console large enough to serve the needs of NASA, its mammoth screen as blank as mine had been a moment earlier. If this was a movie (though nothing seemed to move), it was not the classic screwball comedy I had a craving for. I pressed the channel selector forward, backward, with no effect on the image I had called up. Retreating to the couch, I tried the remote. Nothing worked, not even the control that would identify the channel that carried such an arty drama workshop, for what else could this still-life production be? Not a word spoken, not one close-up of a face, it certainly wasn't the usual soap that dominated this hour on TV.

Curious as to how long they would dare to occupy the screen with a silent sedentary character who showed only his back, I watched in growing fascination, thinking what an easy script for an actor to learn—nothing to do but fiddle with those dials. At last some action—in a sudden fit of pettishness, he leaned forward and gave his screen a sharp smack. Immediately an image flashed on and instinctively I smiled at the use of my own childish technique for bringing a recalcitrant machine to order.

The image he had summoned up was vaguely familiar—a blonde in her late thirties or early forties, with the close-lipped smile of someone with no confidence in her dentist. Not much to look at. She ought to do something with that hair, at least wash it. Only for a split second did I see that face just so. Then I felt the same cold prickling under the skin that I have felt when I have just escaped being run over by a car. That was *me*! The back presented to the camera stiffened into alertness. The man slapped his desk in apparent delight. "Hello, hello," he murmured as if to himself, "now where do you come from, I wonder?"

Somewhere, at some time, they had taped me, was the obvious explanation and I began to rage at this unconstitutional invasion of privacy. At the same time I could not tear my eyes away from my own image. Just as I had seen the smile dissolve into panic, so I now saw the panic corrode into anger. This was no tape, this was a *live* production! All my stunned brain could imagine was that this was one of those supposedly funny home videos designed to make the audience feel not only smarter but thinner. No point in asking how, without cameras, light, wiring—everyday there was some technological advance that made possible the impossible—but why was still a good question. Especially why hadn't I washed my hair, or picked up the papers, or chosen something else to wear but a tee shirt and jeans?

"Don't tell me your era now, let me guess," came the coy injunction from the man on the screen. Not my age, my era, mind you. I upped the already astronomical sum I was deciding to sue them for. "The latter part of the twentieth century? Early twenty-first?"

Suppose the jury awarded me five million, the judge struck it down to two, even one—that would pay for a real certified nanny with enough left over for a cleaning service—the kind where a cadre of men come in like stormtroopers and leave a devastation of cleanliness in their wake...

The time, the time, he kept asking, as if there were no clock at his studio. Still thinking of my lawsuit, I warned myself to give no evidence of cooperation, say nothing. "I must know the time," he pleaded. He made it sound so urgent, I gave in.

"12:28 p.m." I made a point of being exact.

But it was the date, the date he wanted to know. It was beginning to sound like a sanity test. "January 18," I said and added sarcastically, "Shall I also give you the name of the president of the United States?"

"Your president is of no moment. Just the year, the year," he pleaded, and when I gave him the year, he gasped.

"As early as that? My God, a genius, an unknown genius, and a female one at that! How many like you, I wonder, have been edited out of the written records by the Neanderthal males of your era? You seem to have hit on the time-accelerator 300 years before Chiu Li, but he got the credit."

I simpered—a purely automatic response—but quickly wiped off the silly smirk evident on his screen. For the purposes of my lawsuit, I had to remember not to look pleased.

"But you probably don't know *my* date," he suddenly cried. "My name hardly matters, of course—" and, of course, he proceeded to give it with some pomposity. Protonstein, it sounded like. "What you want to know is the time you've hit. Well, this is January 18, 2519."

I knew damn well it was January 18, I had told him as much, thereby proving I was in full possession—

"Two thousand, five hundred, nineteen," he spelled out considerately. "Is that what you have the accelerometer set for?"

I blacked out. At least, I think I did. When I opened my eyes again, there he was, still leaning forward toward his screen, patiently awaiting an answer. "Ah ha, you are surprised," he laughed, wagging his finger. "Had it set for another century, eh? Don't be embarrassed, it happens even today sometimes. And the decelerometer is even more unreliable."

He was being pityingly kind, I could tell, not criticizing the give-or-take-a-century inaccuracy of my primitive machine. I burst into hysterical laughter. He must have mistaken it for restored good humor.

"You interview me first," he suggested, "since if any-thing happens to the connection, the present has the advantage over the past." A little gesture of gallantry re-minded me which was which. "So ask your questions," he said and leaned back receptively.

Silence. Ask your questions, this apparition from the future cried, and I could think of nothing to ask.

"I understand," he said soothingly, "so many problems your century had, seemingly insoluble, you find it difficult to choose which should take precedence. Relax, take the first that comes to mind."

Is this for real, was the only question my dazed mind could formulate. Ask something, ask anything, I prodded it—that's the only way you'll find out. I repeated his advice: relax, take the first thing that comes to mind. "What about the servant problem?" I heard myself squeak. With that bit of silliness ringing in my ears, a wish-I-was-dead embar-rassment washed over me.

I wanted to explain the state of my mind. And while I was about it, the state of my dress, the state of my house, the state of my hair. But he gave me no chance.

"Madam!" he exclaimed, no longer leaning back relaxed but sitting stiffly upright. "Madam! I see we shall waste no time. Without preamble you strike at the basic problems."

At that remark, I felt a strong need to view the expres-sion on his face. As sarcasm, it was certainly heavy-handed, and even sarcasm implied more comprehension than I had thought likely. Surely mankind in 500 years would have so computerized life that the very word "servant" would have been long obsolete. But when he continued, there was no mistaking his seriousness.

"Yes, we have outlawed war, eradicated poverty, repaired the environment, colonized space so that overpopulation is no longer a concern—we have even stamped out smoking!—but the servant problem—there you have us."

My heart sank, though a promised solution in 500 years should hardly have made it leap for joy.

"I know what you are going to say," he quickly forestalled any response from me, "and it's true that almost everything now is done by machine.—electronic, nucleonic, bionic. Once we replaced silicone with DNA, we thought there was no problem our computers would find insoluble. There are even anti-matter devices to *undo* work, and believe me, they have come in handy at times. But what is the result? More servant jobs than ever before and less servants. Who wants to spend his life waiting for lights to flash, pushing buttons, emptying nuclear waste, or signaling for catastrophe squads when some gadget gets out of order?"

"It does sound idiotic," I agreed.

"Exactly. We thought of that too, and naturally assigned the mentally deficient to do it. But with genetic engineering what it is today, there aren't many of those left. Of course in big industry, the computers serve well but in the field of personal services and in the home, we're stuck—we had to go back to mothers for children, by the way."

"Then there is no hope?" Mine was the lugubrious tone reserved for addressing ravens who croak "nevermore."

"Well," came the judicious reply, "I wouldn't say that. Pillmacher and I—she's a colleague of mine—thought we had it licked not so long ago. Everyone thought so, there was even talk of awarding us the Order of Great Magnitude. My wife had already—" There was a moment of silence while he seemed wistfully to finger the broken shards of this dream. With an obvious effort, he called his mind back to the present reality.

"It happened," he began, "when Pillmacher and I received reports on a newly discovered planet in the Northeast. As you know, that part—but of course you don't know," he interrupted himself, "anyway, that part of the galaxy is almost never traversed because of the intense magnetic storms. This ship was off its course, had lost its way; by pure chance it landed where it did, and by pure luck it managed to navigate safely back.

"Our job is to interview returning personnel of any exploratory task force, coordinate their reports, etc. and we were mildly excited at the news of this flight's return since it would help fill in what was still a lamentably blank area on our map. But when we had the captain up, we could get little but a verbal description of the place. None of his instruments had worked. The planet seemed to be an insignificant one, similar to Earth. Very much so, according to the flora he had recorded. As for fauna, he had brought back specimens of the lower life forms that would make interesting zoo exhibits and two—a male and a female—of the highest developed species.

"Funny creatures they were, similar to humans but with certain intriguing variations. Because of their very similarity, they seemed more monstrous than the intelligent Things and Blobs we had previously encountered in outer space. The head was almost square, the facial features flattened to one plane. Their eyes were dog-like, filled with the dark iris, showing only corner patches of white. The mouth, open or closed, stretched in a grimace that we interpreted as a grin. The arms and legs were paired off symmetrically, positioned just as ours, but at the elbow the brachium sprouted into two forearms, each ending in a perfectly functioning five-fingered hand.

"They had already developed a pidgin version of our language, and we noted that their vocal sounds were sustained, rising and falling in a melodic line—such a merry-sounding one to our ears that we found ourselves chuckling irrepressibly even when they were telling us of their fright and loneliness.

"After a brief preliminary interview, we sent them to the personnel testing laboratory for further observation and study. The fellows there were delighted with them. It was a relief, after all, to find one intragalactic being that was not more intelligent than we are. They have a tough job down there, I feel for them, with even the vegetables from some planets outthinking them. But here they were for once with a chance to test somebody, instead of being tested, as things so often turned out.

"I don't know who had the great idea first, Pillmacher or I. I would say we thought of it at the same time, when we saw the lab's report a month later. It started off, as such reports do, with the I.Q. Rather low, male 110, female 120, "similar to man's prior to introduction of triphosphocogitine in diet, Probably can be raised by dietary supplement?" That I remember verbatim, question mark and all.

"Manual dexterity, the report proceeded to note, was excellent, they were quadridextrous. As for temperament, the slight homesickness had been quickly dispelled, after which they had remained monotonously cheerful, even placid, under the most taxing test situations.

"Certain specific physiological information awaited autopsy but along with the usual clinical data were a few notes of particular interest: sleep requirement, two hours a day; caloric intake, amazingly low; physical activity, incessant. The need to keep busy was underlined as a deep-seated emotional force—they became moody and depressed otherwise. As for their character traits, they revealed an archaic constellation: trustworthy, loyal, helpful, friendly, courteous, kind, obedient, morally straight, cheerful, thrifty, brave, clean and reverent to all psychologists. Aptitudes? They seemed to have but one. Machinery.

"Without the need for one explanatory word to each other, Pillmacher and I cancelled all appointments and rushed down to the testing lab to confirm the resplendent possibilities dawning before us. Knowing that tests can produce artifacts in behavior as in anything else, we decided to follow them about for several hours and watch the normal routine of their day.

"The menial staff of that department, with the low cunning peculiar to their kind, had already seized upon the salient point. Wherever the creatures wandered—and they had free run of the place now—they took over the work. They ran the power plant, the laundry, the sprayers, the sterilizers. Visiting a latrine, they came upon a ward attendant cleaning up and gleefully took over that job too. We watched them turn on the flood switch, direct the scourer, push the buttons for water evaporation, while the attendant reclined lazily on a stool, reading a comic book.

"The book, I noticed, bore the imprint of the Cygnus colony. That came as no surprise. We rely heavily on imported labor, you see—the pay is good enough to attract them and they can have quite a nest egg when they return home. When I reprimanded the man sharply on allowing inmates to do his work, he looked at me sullenly and with the uncouthness one has learned to expect from colonials, spat on the shining floor. 'They think it's a high honor,' he sneered, although *high* was not the adjective he used.

"With a handshake, Pillmacher and I silently congratulated each other. This was the final confirmation. Honor, yes, there's the rub. Without honor, who is a man? With honor, who is a servant? There have been only two ways to recruit such a class: you, for example, browbeat it into serving by your economic system; we, more civilized, prefer the bribe. An easier, better-paying job you cannot find today, but do people rush to apply? They do not. Oh, we get a few—the dull-witted or the dull-souled. But even they are capable of dull resentment. No, there's no honor in it and nothing we've been able to do has put honor in it.

"Yet here were beings—not human, but twice as dexterous—who thought it an honor to do these menial chores. Tetramanus, humanoid, riant, antidromic, Lamarkian laborers—so the guys at the lab had labelled them. Easier to use the initials and call them THRALLS. It was as THRALLS we checked them out and took them home—Pillmacher the male, I the female—for a month's trial. If that worked out, then we would set the wheels in motion.

"You couldn't find a better test situation. Having large families, we both have spacious living quarters and quite a bit of land. Space, of course is no longer at a premium since the Mass Exodus to other planets, except during the tourist season when the colonials come trouping back to see old mother Earth. You can see that with all that space and all those kids, a servant like this was a godsend.

"It was pure heaven, that first month with the THRALL in the house. In less than a week she knew how to operate everything, could follow faithfully any recipe, took to gardening like a duck to water, and had the kids so well in hand we accused them of being enTHRALLED.

"Happy, the kids named her, and happy she was. That was what made it so perfect. What a pleasure it was to see her flat smiling face, to hear her singing away merrily, while with her four hands she did the work so efficiently we had to manufacture odd jobs to keep her happily busy.

"The male at Pillmalcher's proving equally satisfactory, we rolled up our sleeves and planned Operation Thralldom. Of the first ten freighters we sent out, six were unable to locate the planet, two were lost, but two returned in due course with full cargoes. Those first two shipments, I must confess, were obtained by sheer abduction, but subsequently we were able to send back trained THRALLS as recruiting agents. Full of enthusiasm themselves, they had no trouble in imparting it to their fellow beings and from that time on we legally contracted for their services.

"Our terms were liberal, you must admit. At the end of each year's service, they were free to sign up again, to remain on Earth as full citizens in any other capacity for which they were qualified, or to return home. They were free to choose, we said, knowing full well that for such as they, there was no choice but servitude.

"As a matter of fact, it became an international holiday—Signing-Up Day—with all contracts terminating and being renewed on April lst, the day the first two THRALLS had arrived on Earth. It was a wild carnival that we looked forward to all year. We humans wore squared-off masks and strapped on an extra pair of plastic arms, and for one day acted their part. They good-naturedly donned egg-shaped heads, strapped up two hands, and mimicked our human occupations, being so energetically idle (as they saw it) that they had hangovers for a week afterwards.

"Those were wonderful times, that first decade. We continued to discover some physiological peculiarities but these seemed only to fit them more closely to their menial role. Perhaps because of the magnetic forces of their home planet, their life-span was less than half ours, yet they seemed to not age; they bore litters of five to ten, and the new generation gave every sign of maturing in one decade. We immediately stopped all further importation, to avoid the classic dilemma of the sorcerer's apprentice, and sat back to enjoy the fruits of the labor of that second generation.

"The second generation. That was the crux of the matter, but who could have known? Fortunately I myself had the first twinge of foreknowledge and in the end was the one to explode the myth we ourselves had created—the myth of the perfect servant. I shudder even today to think of the humiliation had Pillmacher and I received the Order, and *then* the truth had come out.

"At least I pride myself on how quickly I grasped the situation. Pillmacher too had her place overrun with little THRALLS and yet she noticed nothing. I was in the solarium, I remember, doing my regular morning exercises, when I noticed one of Happy's little sons—which one I couldn't tell, they all look alike, you know. I was immediately uneasy without knowing why. Suddenly it occurred to me that the young rascal wasn't doing anything. Just sitting there. Not moving a muscle in any of his four arms.

"What are you doing? I asked. Nothing, he mumbled. Nothing! Children are such mimics, I tried to reassure myself. Come, come, lad, I said heartily, you must be doing *something*. Well, if you must know, he replied—and where was the melodic singing voice, where the cheerful grin—I am just thinking.

"Thinking. There you have it in a nutshell. Still I refused to face reality, hoping against hope that I was being overly imaginative. I asked the little tyke to set up the massaging unit and he did, but slowly, reluctantly almost, using only two of his arms I noticed, and those with a most unTHRALL-like fumbling. I had never seen such an expression on the face of a THRALL before. It was downright sullen.

"Wasn't his head just a little less square than it should have been? The features in sharper relief? And those two arms that he didn't use, wasn't there something wrong with them, weren't they shrunken? The boy was a sport, I told myself frantically, a freak mutation caused by the higher radioactive content of our atmosphere. But we were not offered this easy way out. When I alerted Pillmacher, she too found that out of ten youngsters her THRALL had so far fathered, there were three secretly engaged in thinking (brooding would be the better word for it), five were growing closer to the physical form of humans even if mentally they seemed still okay, and the rest in slight but ominous ways differed also from their parents.

"An international survey of the situation only confirmed our worst premonitions. The second generation was forsaking the ways of their parents. The race, contaminated by its new environment, was losing all its intrinsic virtues. Another generation or so and they would be indistinguishable from us. We had overlooked one fact, one fatal fact: Humanity is contagious."

The silence that fell on us both was of infinite sadness. What was it in our species that made close contact so dangerous even for such alien life forms, imprinting them with our own stiff-necked genes, leaving them riddled with discontent, pocked with rage?

In my distress, I wanted more than the back of a head to commune with, however comfortably familiar it had become. I suddenly remembered that Richard had left early to get a haircut—I could now tell him that in the year 2500-whatever, he needn't bother, straggly was the style.

"Do turn around, won't you?" I urged, and he was just beginning to do so when the doorbell rang. There was a blinding flash, a quivering of wavy lines, exploding color— and then the screen was blank.

"Well, my dear," my mother-in-law smiled wearily, looking her age, "I've brought Sally back a little early, I'm afraid, but I've just remembered an appointment."

I must have still looked dazed because she broke off her apologies to ask if anything was the matter. The matter? Yes, something was the matter. But nothing I saw fit to tell her. Or Richard either, I decided. What was the point, when there was no hope for it—now or in the future.

MYSTERIES

HIS FATHER MADE IT SOUND AS WHOLESOME AS COOKED cereal in the morning. "There's nothing like fresh air and country living," said the powerful figure effulgent in summer shirting as he hoisted Boone's duffel bag onto the luggage rack. Exactly what he had said the night before when Boone announced he didn't want to go. To which he had added (Boone's mother venturing to suggest ten was too young, a great-uncle and great-aunt too old) that it would be a valuable learning experience. None of which made four weeks on a farm sound like much of a vacation. Good Humor trucks, stickball in the streets, firecrackers in the park, hand-to-hand combat with wet towels along the slippery edge of city pools, the jerky stop-and-stop wending

homeward from the beach on traffic-jammed Sundays—
those were the proper treats of summer.

Almost in tears, Boone sought to wave goodbye from
the window of the slowly gliding train, but his father had
not stayed, was even then being borne aloft at a stately but
inexorable pace. Years later, studying the Greeks, Boone
was to recognize the machine that lowered and raised the
god on stage as the Union Station escalator.

To any child the first trip from home is an interplane-
tary journey, and in fact Boone's remembrance in those
later years could have been mistaken for a lunatic recounting by some crackpot claiming to have been abducted by a
UFO. A world of purple trees and yellow sky. Weird beings
with metal objects sprouting from their heads. Aunt Flo
was reduced in time to that: steel-grey hairpins popping
out of steel-grey hair. And Uncle Eban to a porkpie hat.
But the house, the house he remembered in all its Queen
Anne glory, a result no doubt of all those hours spent lying
on his back in a field that seemed a level plain when he
stood erect but which betrayed a definite declivity when he
threw himself supine—a saucer on whose rim were aligned
all the taller structures of the farm. There the barn, whose
cool interior smelled half of stable, half garage. There the
longer, lower shed that stank of pure cow. There the
wooden silo, a listing barrel that had burst its staves. There
the metal one, nosing the sky like a rocket on a launching
pad. And there the house.

Long after the features of Aunt Flo and Uncle Eban
had become an amorphous blur, he could recall every aspect of that jumbled pile, every scallop, filligree and furbe-

low, every crazy angle of separate pitched roofs varying in direction of their axes according to the whim of each new generation. And rising above them all, the topmost little roof, fitting like a conical cap—the crow's nest with its oval eye of colored glass.

That was such a place from which a child plucked from the civic hearth and perched on high might witness the great and unspeakable, initiand to Eleusinian Mysteries.

"Did you have fun?" his father asked, forcefully as was his wont, when Boone returned looking, as his father said, fit as a fiddle, covered with wholesome scabs and scratches.

"No," said Boone. After so long an abstinence, ambrosial was the smell and taste of take-home pizza. "There weren't any other kids around, they don't even have TV."

"It's high time you learned to manufacture your own entertainment," his father said, and his mother nodded yes, yes, yes. Boone had never thought of fun before as a skill to be learned, like tying shoelaces.

Stretching out then tonguing up the rubbery strings of cheese, Boone wondered if he should tell his parents the kind of entertainment people manufactured when they didn't have TV. The game Aunt Flo and Uncle Eban played of an evening was mostly picking him apart, vying with each other at finding fault. Don't tell me that's all you eat at home, you'll never reach a man's full growth. Don't tell me your ma just packed you shorts, bare legs won't do for walking through them fields. Don't tell me you just had your hair cut, you'll be taken for a girl. Don't tell me you don't go to church—We was just funning, Aunt Flo explained, when he broke down and cried.

"And did you learn to milk a cow?" his mother asked. The way she leaned forward, elbows on the kitchen table, both hands spread to cup her pointed chin, lent great importance to the question. Boone shook his head, shame-faced admission to a failing grade. He had gone into the cowshed only once, didn't like the smell.

His father laughed. "I don't remember much of my one summer on that farm, but I do remember that—they made me clean it out."

Boone lavished all attention on the last morsel of his pizza as if he doted on burnt crust. No reason he could see to admit that Uncle Eban had tried to make him do the same, but he had hidden until they gave up looking, gave up calling. Either the crow's nest was forgotten or it wasn't worth the climb.

The little round window was of colored glass. Yellow and purple It was midday but through that window the light was forever a dying afternoon's. From his eyrie, Boone looked down on the squashed porkpie hat, never doffed indoors or out. Uncle Eban was cleaning out the cowshed by himself. The usual overalls, flailed into pale blue lifelessness by Aunt Flo's laundering, had been replaced by the old shirt and trousers kept hanging in the shed for just such jobs. The one time he went inside, Boone had brushed against them, jumped back in alarm, not recognizing them as clothes to be worn. On his uncle, mounding the manure into a dark volcanic cone, they seemed made not of cloth but of some old dark metal, heavy and durable as iron, as seasoned in their way as the cast-iron skillet on Aunt Flo's stove.

It was Aunt Flo's entrance that gave the scene a disconcerting turn. She was wearing a too-large raincoat of smoky transparency, strange stuff that reminded Boone of the isinglass windows on the ancient car rusting in the barn. Why a raincoat, was the puzzle. Boone peered up. Not a cloud in the yellow sky. Not a shadow of a cloud near the purple sun. Squeezed tightly under her arm, a plump chicken squirmed. Its beak took chopstick bites out of empty air. A frisson of terror—or was it delight?—rippled over Boone's skin. He knew, even as the chicken seemed to know, what came next.

I'll wring your neck. Her customary expression of mild annoyance. You track mud over this floor just once again, boy, I'll wring your neck.

Boone remembered back to breakfast, what she had said. Not for you to watch, don't even let the other chickens watch, she had said. All Boone heard from Uncle Eban was a contemptuous expulsion of air through the hairy marshland in his nose, but shut up, Aunt Flo commanded, taking a steel hairpin out of her hair and glaring across the table as if she meant to plunge it into Uncle Eban's heart, stuck it instead into another part of her scalp. It's not like the boy's brought up to it, she said. Take me, it's been my chore since I was eight years old, when Ma got her bursitis. My sister Edna now, she never done it till she was married. You should have seen her, boy, that first time, she left her new husband high and dry, with no supper on the stove, come crying home to Ma and me, all covered with the blood. We thought at first Billy done beat her—with all that carrying on you couldn't make head nor tails of what she said.

Uncle Eban addressed a snort to "your sister Edna," but Aunt Flo's patting of her thick grey hair, her groping for the lethal hairpin was purely automatic. Hers was the foolish out-of-focus smile that grownups wore when remembering good times past. Poor Edna, she had laughed.

Poor chicken. Boone heard the furious pounding of the tiny heart under the feathered breast. It took the silent mouthing of the figures far below to make him realize the heartbeat was his own. They were yelling. The mouths spat and twisted and opened wide in silent roars. He could hear nothing, he was missing all the fight. He wiped the stained glass porthole with his shirttail as if cleaning wax out of his ears. Uncle Eban flung his shovel to the ground and yelled again. One hand still binding tight the chicken's legs, Aunt Flo used her other to tear into her hair, jerking out, jabbing in the pins, her mouth working away. When it happened, it took Boone completely by surprise. Reversing her hold, its head now in her hand, she began to whirl the chicken around and around, the way he whirled his model planes into flight. Oh ho, he's going to get it now, Boone laughed to himself, as silently as those titans cursing each other below—she's going to throw it at him. And so she did.

The chicken took off straight for Uncle Eban, but its head stayed in her hand. Boone saw the reason for the raincoat then. Uncle Eban was soaked with blood, stunned with blood. Aunt Flo's head was far back, her mouth open, drowning in laughter. The chicken kept on going, floundering about the bare yard, a geyser of blood spurting from the open neck, its wings flapping vigorously as if still convinced it could escape in flight. He did not see Uncle Eban plow his shovel into the manure pile but he heard Aunt Flo's scream, faint and shrill as a train whistle miles down the track.

Uncle Eban dripping with blood. Aunt Flo, buttoned up in her raincoat as if forearmed against droppings from the sky, drowning in that other stuff. In her hair, plastered to her face, oozing from her mouth. And the chicken careening around them both, its blood now jetting in a finer spray, a lawn-sprinkler wetting the thirsty earth in a time of drought.

"I learned how to kill a chicken," Boone said to his mother, who had shown her disappointment that he hadn't learned to milk a cow. He felt resentful when she made a face. It was a learning experience, he would have thought.

His father took it more in stride. "Okay, so you can kill a chicken, hot stuff. What else did you learn?"

Boone opened his mouth to tell them, then shut it tight. There is no child so young he does not know what happens to those who witness the unspeakable and bring back a report.

PIGEONS

ANOTHER DEAD PIGEON. THE THIRD THAT WEEK. THIS one Talitha turned over carefully, using a stick, avoiding any touch, for Maurice had impressed upon her that they were carriers of disease. Like the others, it showed no external injury, not even the effects of a fall. It lay there still plumped out with apparent health, the feathers a little ruffled, lacking their customary sheen, like a specimen of the taxidermist's art which had too long gathered dust on a shelf and finally been thrown out.

Anything but pigeons, she would not have given it another thought. Carcasses were common on city streets, but not old pigeons that had died as uneventfully as these. Hearing Maurice's beautifully articulated voice—"and do you know how to tell the age or give a proper medical examiner's report?"—she strove for more exactness: before this week she had never seen the unmangled corpse of a mature pigeon of whatever age.

And so she remarked to Maurice when she saw that he was unimpressed by the mortality statistics she reported. It *was* strange, she insisted, you just don't see old pigeons lying about. Babies, yes. Those poor little things, still unfeathered—a terrible blue nakedness—with pop eyes and wobbly necks, flattened on the sidewalks, sometimes with an explosion of gory innards from the impact of the fall. She had often wondered where the old ones went to die, for surely they got old, had heart attacks, varicose veins, became too arthritic to fly and had a senile fit of forgetfulness on a ledge twelve stories up. That "surely" was but a preface to a doubt: perhaps they never knew old age and only accident and disease kept their population within bounds. Unless perhaps, like elephants, they had a secret burial ground?

Maurice corrected her about the elephants. Ah, you know everything, her adoring look told him. Which was why, true seeker after knowledge but not much of a reader, she had dropped out of college to marry him. Elephants, she learned now, do not wander off to some particular spot to die. That was a myth. Such graveyards as are found contain the bones of elephants of all ages, clearly the remains of a herd decimated by disease. But about the pigeons, he had nothing much to say beyond remarking that one pigeon looked so much like another she might well be counting and recounting the same dead bird.

She doubted that. "Do you suppose someone is poisoning them?" Pigeons had their ardent supporters, mostly old ladies who lived alone, having amassed a lifetime's savings of crumbs, but they had their detractors too, equally ardent, who would like to see their breasts impaled on iron spikes and were no doubt capable of strewing poisoned grain alas on the grass.

"Am I to assume you number yourself among the pigeon-lovers?" Maurice asked with an ironical lift of one brow, an eighty-year habit which had imprinted on his forehead an acute tilt of wrinkles as if underneath lay some geological fault.

"Well—" she temporized, not willing to commit herself, "I do admire their success in adapting to urban life."

"By the same reasoning," Maurice said, with the entirely different arrangement of wrinkles appendant to his smile, "you must like rats."

Talitha could see that pigeons did not arouse his ardor, pro or con. Still, her mention of poison must have caught his interest, for with the first sound of drums from the park Maurice swore in Switzerdeutch (which, after three years of marriage, still sounded to her like German spoken without dentures), then wished in his enviable English that the civic-minded poisoners would forgo the pigeons, direct their attention to the Sospitians instead. They seemed to have adapted equally well to urban life, he complained.

~~

This was their first summer in the city and they considered themselves fortunate to have found an apartment on a street bordering a large park. Doubly fortunate to have a

corner bedroom with cross-ventilation, since Maurice
could not tolerate air conditioning (his sinuses clogged up)
and it was only the coolness provided by so much greenery
that made sleep possible at all in the present heat. A bit of
serendipity, that, since it had been September when they
bought the co-op, with a spanking freshness in the air and
city trash swirling all about, and all they had thought of
was interior spaces, seeking the high ceilings and generous
dimensions still extant in prewar buildings. Thirty years of
residence in the States gave Maurice the right to call himself American, a right he fully exercised, but he still felt at
home only in surroundings that reminded him of Europe:
mountains with the abrupt grandeur of the Alps, lakes
with the classic contours of Geneva, seashores rocky and
indented as in Brittany. And here along the park was a
divided boulevard, as spacious and tree-lined as the Unter
den Linden he had known in his distant youth.

Not least among the amenities of their new home was
Venus, their Jamaican housekeeper. There is so much one
has to leave behind, the previous owner had sighed, looking
first at the drapes and then at the black and buxom woman
packing her fine china. Do stay on and work for us, they
had pleaded—Maurice enchanted by what a Caribbean lilt
could do for British English, Talitha by the cheerful round-
ness of her face, the mothering promise of that well-
cushioned form.

What a piece of luck, became their matutinal greeting.
"It's like living in a first-class hotel," Maurice said. "I never
see her in my study, I never find a book misplaced, a paper
out of order, yet everything is spotless."

"I knew she would work out when she didn't ask what cleaning things to use," Talitha bragged. Such a relief, not to be required to have strong convictions on the subject of detergents.

At the beginning, included in their good fortune were the Sospitians, whose occupancy of several smaller, older buildings across the street had brought the price within their reach. Coloreds, the agent had called them, scrupulous in forewarning them of undesirable neighbors. While Talitha was still considering that descriptive term—to her ears more South African than American—Maurice spoke up, taking (as he would have said) the bull by the balls. "Let us call a spade a spade," he said. Only death has bred more euphemisms than the real estate trade, he later contended. Talitha agreed but at the moment wished he would remember English was not his native tongue and be more circumspect in taking idioms by the horn. Oblivious to the agent's shock—that of a poor innocent who had dared a mild off-color joke only to be rebutted with pure smut—Maurice went on to assure the man in his precise Oxbridge style that he and his wife were not at all averse to cohabiting with blacks. Horrors! the agent's gesture cried, open palms vigorously erasing dirty words from the air. Their neighbors did not belong to that morose American species but were of a gentler Caribbean persuasion. Not black at all, just —colored, he resorted to again. And so they were, Talitha discovered to her surprise. Theirs was a color that made the stereotypical racial pigmentations look too black, too brown, too white, too yellow, not enough red. How did they come by such a color, she wondered enviously. It was like skin that received none but beneficent rays from the sun.

But with summer came a nightly convocation of Sospitians on the edge of the park and the sound of their drums was driving Maurice mad. Talitha did not mind it so much; when it first started up, she would listen for a while, trying to plot the complicated beat, but the pattern was so unvarying, the tempo so unchanging she was soon no more conscious of it than of the variation in pitch of the revolving fan as it turned toward then away from their enervated bodies on the bed, her nakedness bared to the oscillating breeze, his modestly enshrouded in the sheet.

For Maurice the very repetitiveness was a torture, worse than a faucet drip. "But faucet drips aren't so bad," Talitha tried to soothe him, "if you let it, the plop-plop-plop can actually put you to sleep."

More irritably than was his wont, Maurice corrected her again: not all faucets accommodated the nerves with so steady a drip; there was also the faucet that went plop-plop—and then nothing, a black hole of silence, while a trickle of water pushed its way through the pipes, welled up in its throat, ballooned from its mouth, to drop at last with a thunderous PLOP. It was that excruciating breath-holding, saliva-pooling wait that kept sleep at bay and so with this drumming: his whole body tensed, awaiting the occasional "break," that came as unpredictably as a missed heartbeat, bringing with it the same tremor of alarm.

"I know just the thing!" Talitha cried, snapping her fingers in self-approval. "Earplugs! I'll get you a pair tomorrow."

The earplugs worked. Maurice, who had balked at first at such undiscriminating deafness, in due time confessed himself delighted. "Three good night's sleep in a row!" he crowed, equally delighted with his morning erection. He hooked a finger in Talitha's mouse-colored hair. "That's why I married you," he said, pulling her to him by the baby-fine strands.

"To get a good night's sleep?" she asked, with the innocent look that tickled him so. His head moved forward, the chin tilted up, as if to keep his smile, faint as it was, from spilling over. She was reminded of a cat she once had, who struck that pose whenever she stroked it under the chin.

"Not for *that*," he said, treating her to the twinkle usually reserved for a larger audience (he was at his most flirtatious when leaning over a lectern and speaking to a full house). "We make a good fit, my dear. There are problemposers, such as I, useful only to the world at large, and there are problem-solvers, such as you, my dear, which is exactly what one needs about the house."

There developed a new problem that Talitha could not solve. Maurice often forgot to remove the earplugs in the morning and Talitha forgot he had them in. Breakfast conversation could not but languish when cheerful remarks received no response or at best were answered with non sequiturs. That this might be a preview of senility was to Talitha a new and frightening thought. Asking her not to mumble, Maurice had much the same fear.

One evening, taking the earplugs from the little jewel-box Talitha had provided, he held them doubtfully in his hand and puzzled aloud over his reluctance to insert them.

"Can it be that somewhere in here"—he tapped his head—"there exist vestigial remnants, a diseased appendix of primitive thoughts that occasionally flares up into a feverish irrationality? Much as I applaud the effect of these plugs, I cannot put them in without a feeling of dread, as if I were performing a ritual of mimetic magic that might prove only too efficacious in the end."

Talitha pondered his heavy prose. "You mean, like, mockin's catchin'?"

He absorbed that new colloquialism without his usual panegyric on the genius of the English language for brevity and wit. His glumness came as no surprise—it was to be expected of a genius, this roller-coaster life of ups and downs. One day his step was as bouncy as a sneakered kid's and the next he saw himself becoming one of those old men whose wives behave like nannies, always straightening their clothes and wiping the corners of their mouths. Really the most ridiculous fear, she would blithely reassure him, adding for good measure a particularly lascivious kiss, after which, as reinforcement, she would find some way to bring up Stockholm and how many times she had heard him called the youngest of them all, not excluding that round-faced Chinese schoolboy who shared the Physics Prize. This evening she skipped the first two moves, went straight to Stockholm, holding his hands to forestall the insertion of the plugs until she had finished telling him who was the youngest of them all. He looked so much like a little boy who knew he had deserved a scolding that she pulled his head down and kissed him smack in the center of his sunburned pate. And reminded herself she must see to it that he wore a hat when he went out. She loved the smooth hard baldness of his head, so much sexier than straggly wisps of grey, but she was sure it rendered him more vulnerable to the direct rays of the sun.

Earplugs in, eyes closed, Maurice sank into a sensory-deprived world which brooked no entry. Talitha lay beside a corpse, pitied herself, so young, already a widow. And left nothing by her late husband but his insomnia. It was she now who listened as if for two to the nightly drummings. Her whole body had become porous to the sound, its cumulative tension cramping the muscles of her legs, its erratic hesitations reflected in the vagaries of her pulse. In desperation she considered dressing and walking out into the night, walking up and down across the street from the partying in the park until the muggy heat wilted her into sleepfulness.

Yet however deaf to external noise, Maurice still could hear the screams and catcalls of his dreams and fall awake to clutch a shoulder, breast or thigh. What if there were no female part at hand to serve as comfort blanket and sucking thumb? To find her gone, first from bed, then from house—she had a painful vision of a heart attack. Just gone for a walk, she thought of penning, only to foresee the reception he would give her when she returned. This is not a city in which a young female walks at night alone, Maurice had counseled her the night before, had insisted on a cab even for a visit to her friend Diane, who lived a mere four blocks away.

Talitha had protested before giving in. It was true that Diane's block, all renovated brownstones, could be intim-

idating late at night, its emptiness made yet more ominous
by the signs of paranoia that seemed to go with private
ownership—signs warning off the dogs with threat of fines;
signs warning off intruders with threat of dogs; signs warning that the block was patrolled; signs warning that these
cars, these houses were protected by such-and-such alarms.
But on this block, to which the Sospitians had restored a
stoop-life, a street-life, with all those brown bodies extrud-
ing from the windows, loitering in the doorways, seeking
yet more lebensraum along the edges of the park, Talitha
felt completely safe.

Maurice had raised a brow at that pronouncement; he
had heard rumors that in those crowded doorways drugs
were being dealt.

Rumors, Talitha scoffed. She had heard rumors too, of
everything from Aids to voodoo rites, had checked them
out with Venus. (In so short a time had Venus become the
authoritative source for happenings on their block. Just the
information gleaned in a laundry room was awesome, Talitha
learned, half-tempted to do the wash herself one day.)

Voodoo? Not bloody likely, Venus had said, busily
chopping vegetables for a stew. "They're nothing like the
Haitians and they'll be the first to tell you so."

Chop chop went the knife so forcefully that a piece of
carrot was projected across the room.

"You don't like them, do you?" a disappointed Talitha
asked, retrieving the carrot and tossing it in the sink.

"It's nothing to do with me," Venus shrugged. "But I'll
tell you how I see it—what they don't like about the
Haitians is not the voodoo, it's the black skin."

It's everything to do with her, Talitha thought, surprised that anger could mottle even the blackest skin.

"All I know," she said to Maurice, "is that I could walk down this street alone at night without the slightest fear."

Maurice took off his glasses, beamed admiringly at the workings of the female mind. It was like watching a little girl in tutu pirouetting around the room, he complimented his bride: she kept her opinion fixed on a certain point and thus could turn and turn and turn full-circle around the facts without becoming dizzy. He had also noticed the more unfounded the opinion, the stronger it was voiced.

Although nettled, Talitha found it hard to justify her confidence in the Sospitians, based as it was on nothing more than their good looks and their speaking French—a patois, of course, but still French. Who could fear assault or rape from those who spoke so civilized a tongue? This she truly believed but took care to declaim it with an exaggerated fervor, lending it the protective coloration of a joke.

Maurice tilted his brow, portrayed himself as astonished. Where was she during the Algerian war? Had she so soon forgotten those less-than-civilized Gallic tortures? The brow came down abruptly. He had remembered where she was— not yet born.

Talitha sulked. The man had no sense of humor. She fell back on a high-minded mulishness, as if the inability to defend her conviction proved it an axiomatic truth. This gave Maurice the pleasure of looking pained and calling her "your generation," an epithet which Talitha hated. It made of her youthfulness something spurious, more a measure of ignorance than years.

"I am aware" he said, " that your generation has for-
sworn the rational, gives credence only to succubi and
chimeras, otherwise known as 'feelings.' But where your
safety is concerned, I must put my foot on it and insist that
you take reasonable care."

And then hoping to dissolve her resistance before it
had congealed into a harder set, he went over to the cross-
legged figure on the couch, took possession of her hand to
stop that biting of the nails. He didn't mind the bitten nails
so much as the clacking of her teeth. She might have been
a young glossy primate grooming herself of fleas.

"Perhaps I too am guided by my feelings," he said,
"more than I would like the world to know. How they
would laugh at such a hoary theme—an old man's love."

The word "love" had melted her then; melted her now.
She abandoned all thought of sneaking out, but still felt
impelled to leave a bed which had become a sounding
board. She got up quietly, forgetting that Maurice could
not hear her, and put on a dressing gown, all romantic
froth, bought just to please him. She found his aversion to
plain nakedness usefully kinky—she herself was never
aware of her body until she had clothed it—and by this
transparent device affirmed her standing as good wife,
accommodating him even in his sleep.

In his study, with door closed, she scanned the shelves
for something to read. Almost anything here, she thought,
should make her eyes heavy. She squatted down to the low-
est shelf where the books were too large to stand upright
and lay on their sides, undoubtedly the weightiest. On top
was a world atlas, which reminded her she still knew noth-

ing about the island home of their neighbors. Venus claimed, with obvious satisfaction, to have never heard of it. For once, even Maurice's store of information proved wanting. He too had never heard of it before encountering its expatriates—a true case of ignorance being bliss. Following his advice, given waspishly, she had turned to the encylopedia, which denied its existence by refusing it an entry. It was therefore in a defeatist frame of mind that she opened the atlas and turned to the index; with all the world to be mapped, it was hardly likely that notice would taken of a place so small and insignificant. Yet there it was, longitude and latitude in italics, page number in bold. With something of the excitement of a Balboa, she found the page. A large detail of the Caribbean, mostly blue water. The lazy arc of islands looked like stepping stones on which one could walk, teetering here and there for balance, all the way to South America. Following the given coordinates, her finger came to rest on one of those off-line pebbles, too small to stand on, too small even on this blown-up scale, to bear a name. Ste. Sospice, she cried out in triumph, as if planting a flag.

~~

The next morning Maurice emerged from his study a rejuvenated man. His work was going well, Talitha thought, her own spirits rising. But, in fact, the battle he had won was against a meaner foe.

"Welkin just called, they have given in, agreed to all my terms," he said, tilting his chin at her.

Welkin: lawyer, tax accountant, agent, general factotum. But who *they* were, Talitha for the moment could not recall. "Oh," she cried when it came to her, "you're going to do the Cyrus Evans interview! You're really going on TV!"

He took a moment to relish her delight. "Yes, I now enter the ranks of the Rich and Famous. I shall be recognized on the street. I shall have groupies following me. I shall be treated with respect by maîtres d'. Even the tellers at my bank will be able to identify me. I know such fame is fleeting, but I shall demand the full five minutes Mr. Warhol has allotted to me."

Talitha did not allow her pleasure to be diluted by his teasing. "I think you've got fifteen minutes," she said absently, her thoughts still on the network superstar. To appear on one of Cyrus Evans' hour-long specials was a validation of greatness besides which the Nobel paled, yet until now Maurice had refused all such offers. Television was not a medium for ideas, he maintained, but for flickering moments that capture the eye, much as a mobile above an infant's crib.

The terms which had given Mr. Evans pause brought Talitha to full stop. "Here?" she said with voice aquiver and looked about the room in dismay. "I thought they filmed those interviews in a studio."

She shrank from making a public display of the Victoriana which was Maurice's taste—the heavy European furniture that for half a century had followed him from place to place, the walls papered from head to foot with photographs, framed memorabilia, and time-blackened landscapes by obscure 19th-century artists, who Maurice assured her had been well-known in their day and would come into their own again.

"Yes, here," Maurice said proudly. "And live, not on tape. That way we have an equal chance of being made a fool. Of course I used a different arguing point. Thus, I said, would he inherit the mantle of the Great One." A look at Talitha and he added, "Mr. Murrow." No enlightenment in her stare. "I am forgetting how short a span to time this five—no, fifteen—minutes is. I suppose your generation has never heard of him."

"Of course I have," Talitha said, coming to, having decided she and Venus must do what they could with the room. "I'm just surprised that you have. You always said you never watched TV."

"My dear, I *knew* him. In London. He interviewed me during the war. On radio, need I say?" He hesitated: which war, need he say? "But that is neither here nor there. Suffice it to say I had Mr. Evans so intent on recreating a classic, he was ready to forswear even color. I was not. Without color, one sees the pure line, and I have too many."

Talitha recognized her cue. "You're thinking of that awful photograph in the Times," she scolded him, referring to the unflattering view taken from the wings of the stage at his last lecture series. It was the lighting, the angle of the shot, she had explained and tore it up. As, she reminded him, she had done with the awful one of her they had printed—an indecipherable face vaporous in clouds of veiling, snapped outside the church after the wedding. It might have been any bride. The only thing to do with a bad picture is not look at it, was her advice then and now. She eyed him cautiously and dropped her gaze.

"When I was a kid," she began (and Maurice smiled at a tone of voice that set the story in such a mythical time), "I was a terrible liar. I mean, I lied a lot. But even when they caught me at it, I wouldn't admit it. The closest I would come was to say, well, maybe I had *exaggerated*. Okay, so here's the camera pulling that same shit—it never lies, it just exaggerates."

"Alas, so does old age," Maurice replied and dismissed the subject with a regal gesture of the hand. A bit like King Canute standing at the water's edge, Talitha thought, and quickly suggested that they celebrate his victory with a picnic in the park.

Maurice liked the idea, generously expanded it to include Welkin and his wife, a couple twice Talitha's age, whom she resented for treating her like a child. An unwanted one at that, Mrs. Welkin managed to imply. In return, Talitha entertained Maurice by deriding the strenuous effort such women made to keep their hold on youth.

"She always looks like one of those runners in a marathon—gaunt-faced, every stringy tendon stretched, coming just abreast the tape," she said from the couch, lazily asprawl.

Maurice laughed. "There is a shorter idiom for that: she makes you tired."

Still they had a pleasant civilized picnic in summer's lingering dusk amid the Victorian fittings Maurice demanded: linen cloth and napkins, real silverware, and a wicker basket in which nestled two chilled bottles of a good white wine. As they approached the park, the Sospitians were already gathering. Talitha cast a curious eye at the three drums left unattended on a bench by the arched entrance—tall cylinders bulging in the middle as if pressured from within by some fermenting liquid. And found time in passing to admire again the color of these people— the warm brown skin of a smoothness that had never known an adolescent's imperfections or even, she suspected, the adult need for a razor's scraping.

Soccer, not baseball, must be their summer game for the men were light-heartedly kicking a ball on the narrow sward of green bordering the avenue—not in serious play but as if to justify the wearing of short shorts, much as women sported on a beach, bikini-clad, with no interest in the water. Those magnificent thighs were sufficient excuse, Talitha thought—like powerful carvings out of some exotic tropical wood. Oh, those were thighs to cling to, to ride upon, to lie between, to be felled by. Jealously she looked back to check out the women, rarely seen in daylight hours. From the odors always drifting down their street, Talitha had concluded they spent all their time in the kitchen. Here too they tended the home fires, sitting apart on the grass, flounced skirts aswirl, hovering over low iron braziers reeking of charcoal and strange spices, a pungent mix of odors that followed her into the park.

By the time the picnickers returned, the drums were going. The women had departed, only the men remained, perched on the backs of the benches, their feet rhythmically tapping the seats. The three drummers were grouped apart under a tree of towering age, whose thick crown formed an inverted cup spilling down on them the full muskmellon ripeness of the summer night.

Maurice stared hard, as if composing a description for the police. He would have left it at that, but the traffic light was long in turning and the drumming at his back began to feel like taunting slaps. Abruptly dropping Talitha's arm, which he always took gallantly before crossing a street, he walked over to the drummers and spoke sharply in French.

"You are fine musicians," he said. "I should enjoy hearing you any time in a concert hall, but not here on the street every night when I am trying to sleep."

Three pairs of hands came to rest on the drum heads, fingers stretched apart as if to equalize the pressure needed to restrain an autonomous power within the drums. It was the middle drummer who answered, in a creole Maurice did not understand. Shifting to the arrogance of English, Maurice asked his name.

"Jean Baptiste," the drummer said so softly that Maurice read him as properly cowed. Talitha's gentle pluck at his sleeve informed him that the light had changed, the Welkins were impatient to cross. He shook off her arm. "And your name?" he asked the other two Sospitians. In any contretemps with underlings, this asking of names was a tactic of intimidation he always found effective. As if, he would thereafter muse delightedly, man still retains the primitive belief that the possessor of his name has him in his power.

"Jean Baptiste," said the second drummer.

"Jean Baptiste," said the third.

"A common name in the Islands," said the middle Jean

Baptiste with a smile directed at Talitha. To Maurice, her answering smile seemed complicitous.

"You are no longer in the Islands," Maurice said in anger, "we have different names here and different manners."

His raised voice brought Welkin quickly to his other side—a man concerned to protect his property—and between his agent and his wife, Maurice's brittle frame was all but carried to the curb, not to be released until the avenue was safely crossed.

"At least I put an end to that infernal noise," he boasted to the departing Welkins. But no sooner had he slammed thir cab door than the drumming started up again. Fumbling with the key to the outer door of their building, he was ashamed to see his hand shaking. Had Talitha noticed? Apparently not. She was still smiling.

~~

How naive she had been, Talitha sighed after the second run-through for the cameras. Being "live," she had assumed, would entail nothing more than taking their seats on the couch and the director calling "roll!" But the last twenty-four hours had kept the entire block in an uproar, with small crowds hovering around the long trailer parked outside, watching the ingress of cables, cameras, mysterious metal boxes, feeding on the rumor that a new network series was being filmed, the names of various TV favorites bruited. Inside, the confusion was just as thick, with hordes of technicians milling about, setting up the lights, testing the sound, installing the air conditioning which Maurice had been prevailed upon to accept for the duration once

Evans had pointed out that, with the windows closed to keep street noises out, the heat from the lights would drown them both in sweat.

Hearing herself exempted from that fate, Talitha was relieved. "You must tell me where I may stand to watch the filming," she interrupted, "I don't want to get in your people's way."

"But my dear," Evans said, exuding charm, "of course you do not stand, you sit. By his side. Except for the final segment when we make a little tour of this delightful room and all the marvelous mementos of his past—then just follow us, you'll be all right."

No sweat, Talitha murmured to herself, accepting her role as part of the domestic interior in which Maurice did his work, thought his great thoughts.

Maurice was not so content. By refusing to be taped or spliced, he had hoped to transform a vulgar medium into a twentieth-century salon. "This is to be a real conversation," he threatened, "with all its bon mots and faux pas, its casuistries and truths—the kind of entertainment no home was once without."

"Your memory fails you there," Evans mildly observed, being of an age to have enjoyed a childhood unblighted by TV. The conversations he remembered were more like shouting matches. Moreover, he warned, there was a script of sorts to be followed: bon mots must not intrude upon commercial breaks and faux pas he preferred to do without.

Air time grew nearer and tension mounted. Venus passed around a tray of sandwiches, waved away by Evans and Maurice, but pounced on by the crew. "I'm going out

for a breath of air," Talitha announced to the room at large.
Only Evans' young assistant heard her and looked around
to shout a warning: "Be back in time for make-up!" Stepping across a mass of heavy cables entwined like copulat-
ing snakes, she made her way into the cool quietness of
the hall, down into the sultry but still comparatively quiet
street. The few gawkers under the building's panoply were
imported whites from other blocks; the Sospitians, siesta-
prone, were rarely visible on late afternoons and even TV
cameras had not induced them to break this rule.

Crossing the avenue, Talitha was surprised to see one
of the drummers, all the more surprised to see him emerging from the park, into which they rarely ventured at any
time of day. She would have thought that, fresh from a
tropical island, they would be drawn to the one site in the
city ever closer approaching a jungle, thanks to municipal
neglect; instead they loitered on their stoops, held convo-
cations against parked cars, and even on picnics restricted
themselves to the strip of green on the hither side of the
park's iron fencing, as if they lacked the proper credentials
to pass through the gate.

Yet here came Jean Baptiste, one hand pressing to his
breast something football-shaped, fresh from playing
some other game than soccer. It *was* Jean Baptiste? she suddenly doubted, then giggled at the doubt, remembering
that the odds certainly favored it. In answer to her smile
of recognition, he drew up before her and she saw the
feathers.

"I know you," he said familiarly, "you were with the
old one."

The missing head emerged from his armpit, startling an "oh" from her. "I thought it was another dead one," she said, following his lead by using her schoolgirl French.

"No, it's very much alive," he said with a smile. "Place your hand here, on the throat, and it will tell you so."

She shrank back. "Pigeons carry disease, I think I should warn you," she said.

His smile broadened. "We find it otherwise," he said. Added more soberly that he spoke of the living—the dead might well be diseased, but their use was forbidden.

"I see," she said. There was a tinge of complacency in her polite smile, for it had struck her how easy was this creole, which Maurice, the great linguist, had found so difficult to understand. "With us, it's lobsters," she graciously volunteered, "which is why I never cook them myself."

He assumed an insulted stance. This was not to eat, he told her loftily, only the blood was used.

Talitha drew in her breath. *Voodoo.* The word seemed to have been voiced outside her head, so intense was the sense of revelation. Immediately she denied that voice: she was confusing these people with the Haitians, for whom they reserved their deepest scorn. Such fine distinctions they make! Venus had said, a certain bitterness in her laugh. Talitha, reporting to Maurice, had laughed too, thereby incurring his disapproval. Fine distinctions were all that separated living matter from the dead, he had instructed her, making her feel foolish.

So she felt now and looked away, then back again, still abashed, her gaze venturing no higher than the pigeon splayed against the open-shirted chest. She reached out a tentative hand, at which the pigeon cocked its head first this way, then that, as if it could see her only from the side. Staring at its curiously flat eyes, Talitha wondered if that was normal for a pigeon or did it have some disease that left intact its peripheral vision while rendering it blind to what lay ahead. Better not touch it, she decided and dropped her hand.

"Those dead ones I've been seeing," she said, following up a minor revelation, "they must be your doing."

He eyed her cautiously. An accusation he had heard before, Talitha sensed, perhaps from one of those old pigeon-lovers with a bag of crumbs. She was just curious, she reassured him, although there was more than curiosity in her rapid shallow breathing and flushed face.

"We try to stun," said Jean Baptiste, "but sometimes by mistake we kill. This one is fine, as you can see." As if to prove the point, he fingered the neck feathers into a ruff. "And tonight there will be good food, good dancing. Would you like to come?"

Though neither he nor she had moved, she felt the distance between them narrowing. "Oh, a party," she said, using the English word, unable to think of the French. "I do love parties." And thought to ask, nodding toward the benches, "Out here?"

He shook his head, pointed to the building facing hers. "A *party*," he said, meticulous repeating her choice of word, "is always held inside."

Almost Talitha said yes. "What am I thinking of?" she cried, "this is the night my husband's on TV. Live, you know." And already on the run, called back, "Channel 4, eight o'clock. Watch it if you can."

The first thing she heard as she edged back into the apartment was her name being called. "I'm here," she answered.

"Oh, there you are," said Evan's assistant. "In those jeans you look like—" he couldn't place what she looked like, settled for—"one of the crew. Better get changed and go for make-up. And your husband's throwing a fit—he wants you."

She went straight to the bedroom, opened the door and stood on the threshold for a moment, the better to appreciate Maurice's antics before the mirror. Trouserless, only a bit of flesh, the ropey tallow of his thigh, exposed between long shirt-tails and high-gartered hose, he was holding to his starched wing collar first a navy blue tie with gold and red stripes, then a solid maroon one, with the same look of fierce concentration he had when approaching a critical point in his work.

"The maroon one," she said.

He gave a startled jump. With the hall light behind her, he could barely make her out. "Oh, it's *you*. Where have you been? I told Evans they shouldn't have let you go, you have no sense of time."

"But I'm here, aren't I?" she said in a chuck-under-the-chin tone of voice.

He could see now her high color and knew where she had been. Soaking up the rays, as she put it, in spite of all his warnings about the damage this would do to her skin.

"Why are you standing there?" he asked, more querulous than ever at such disregard for his advice. "Come tie this for me."

She flipped on the light switch as she entered, knowing that, so long as there was light outside, Maurice would ignore the interior gloom. She was accustomed to his saving ways, which she attributed to his being from another country, and bore with equanimity the accumulation of paperclips and pennies and the post office's daily offering of rubber bands slipped around their first-class mail. Only this battle over light continued to annoy her.

She noosed the strip of maroon around his neck and pulled him to her. "Just who did you think it was—coming into your bedroom without even a knock?" she asked with mock suspicion. A display of jealousy on her part never failed to tickle him into good humor.

"Who? When? Oh, just now? No one in particular."

She saw the crease of satisfaction around his mouth and took credit for it. But he had not really heard her. No one could tie a half Windsor as well as she, he was thinking— a perfect dimple, exactly centered under the perfect knot.

~~

The seconds were ticked off, a light went on, a hand came down, they were on the air. Evans shifted in the armchair, whose placement viz-a-viz the sofa had taken half the afternoon, and spoke with easy directness to the camera.

"Our guest tonight is a man of such protean genius, has left his mark in so many fields of human endeavor, that to list his achievements would take more time than we have. I think it best to confine myself to a few biographical facts and then let him speak for himself. Born ... lived ... studied ... moved ... discovered ... proved ... wrote ... during World War II ... was appointed ... proved ... wrote ...

ventured at the age of 65 . . . was awarded . . . and just this year . . . " Evans cut himself off with a well-rehearsed gesture, charmingly at a loss for words, and focused an inquiring gaze on Maurice. "When I was preparing for this interview, I remember coming to you, sir, and asking just how would you choose to describe yourself—as a scientist, a philosopher, or a writer? You seemed as nonplussed as I. Finally you said, perhaps as just a man with ideas. I certainly can't quarrel with that description—" Evans gave his practiced smile, developed to offset the pugnacious jaw— "but you must admit it doesn't tell me much about where to begin."

Not to be outdone in charm, Maurice leaned forward and twinkled. "Islands," he said, "let us begin with them."

To Talitha came a vision of blue blue water and an arc of small white stepping stones, shattered by Evans' smart cry of Done!—a man striking a bargain.

"Yes, yes, the poet," Maurice said so kindly Talitha knew that, even with the "n" she hastily added, Evans' answer was wrong. "My own association is the Voyage of the Beagle, the Darwinian view of islands as the proving ground for species differentiation. In other words, the birthplace of the unique. So, granted each of us is an island—you see, I give you your poet—with such great oceans between us, each of us knowing only the terra firma of our own sensory experience, what strange creatures we give birth to. We call them ideas. Some of us, more ingenious than others, devise what we hope is a seaworthy bark, load it with one of our miraculous creations (so we see them, yes?) and push it out to sea. The hope is that, after much buffeting by the elements, it may in time reach some other shore. Let us say it does. There the cargo is discovered and, for its very novelty, made much of—but to its creator, were he to see it in that sodden, warped, rusted, splintered, corroded, shattered, stinking state, it would appear a worthless piece of flotsam, intended for God knows what purpose, coming from God knows where."

Evans sensed a put-down but was not sure, having lost Maurice's meaning somewhere in midstream. Feeling a trickle of sweat—was there something wrong with the air conditioner?—he turned to Talitha for light relief. "Do you, by virtue of your marital intimacy, always understand what your husband means?"

Talitha tongued her lips. It was just a multiple-choice, yes or no, not an essay question, she told herself. "Sometimes," she said and smiled brightly.

Maurice patted her hand. "Ours is not a marriage of true minds but of foreign bodies," he said.

Talitha eyed him uncertainly—his smirk implied something obscene. Presented with his profile—the unbroken sweep of brow melding into bald skull, the convex arch of nose, the reptilian slit of eye, the wattled neck emerging from the stiff wing collar, she had the disconcerting thought that Evans was interviewing a Galapagos turtle.

"I know this much," she spoke up strongly, "he's a one and only, maybe that's all he means."

"That much," Evans said briskly, "I too can understand. Nature made him and broke the mold—on that we are agreed." After which, for safety's sake, he took firm control, veering away from any dangerous skirmish with ideas as such, resorting instead to the format fabricated for interviewing movie stars: did Maurice work better in the morning or the night, was it true he had never used a computer, did his ideas take form slowly or did they come in a flash?

Maurice hooded his eyes, thrust forward a clamped jaw. "You mean, under an apple tree or in the bath?" he snapped. "And do I dare to eat a peach or wear the bottoms of my trousers rolled?" Content with Evans' confounded look, he moderated his tone. "I am quite willing to answer all these questions about my personal habits so long as it is understood this conversation is now meaningless. So long as it is understood that the creative process is impervious to explication. I am convinced that whatever is peculiar in the creator is produced by a stochastic event, not even transmitted in the genes—more likely, I have often thought, a mutation occasioned by a hit of radioactivity from outer space."

Talitha nodded, that's true. She was thinking about the genes—his one child was the most ordinary sort of man— a lawyer who lived in Miami and played a lot of golf.

On tape, Evans thought, I would cut him to pieces. Being live, he approached his next question with exquisite politeness. "I hope you will not be offended by a comment on your age, but your vitality makes it seem incredible. Here you are in your eighties—"

"Early eighties," Talitha broke in, much to Maurice's annoyance. It was not a figure he liked to hear repeated.

"Early eighties," Evans accepted her correction, "and yet you give no evidence of slowing down. Do you suppose there is some restorative factor in the process of creativity that accounts for your being so long-lived?"

"Long-lived?" Maurice gave his dry, almost noiseless laugh. "Eighty is not long-lived. Fish are, genetically speaking, long-lived. Pigeons—if you ask my wife." At his teasing glance, Talitha put a finger to her mouth and for lack of nail, frayed a cuticle until it bled. "Coral colonies," he continued smoothly, "and let us not forget cancer cells—the more undifferentiated, the longer-lived are *they*, although, alas, the shorter we. Differentiation is the key, don't you see. Those who wish never to age must strike a very different kind of Faustian bargain: abandon all individuality. Who can tell one carp from another carp, one trout from another trout? Except by size, of course. And there is no reason to believe they would ever cease growing were it not for certain regrettable accidents, such as being eaten by a larger fish."

"Or us," Evans suggested.

"Or us," Maurice agreed. "And yet, even granted the advantages in longevity, who would want to be a fish?"

Talitha, forgetful of the camera, still nibbled on her finger, sucking up the blood. Maurice, not so forgetful, took her hand loverly and asked, "Does that frown mean you have some reservations, my dear?"

"If that is true," she said slowly, playing out the scenario in her mind, "why don't the oceans by now contain just one big fish?"

Evans and Maurice joined forces against her—so she interpreted their laughter. "Did I say something stupid?" she asked, nose in air.

"No, no," Maurice managed to gasp. "There is a Breugel engraving that makes that very point."

Talitha was unappeased. He was still wheezing from the attempt to curtail his laughter. Another resentful look at him and under her makeup Talitha paled.

"Someone please, open a window!" she ordered. "Quickly! He needs fresh air!"

One of the flunkies sidled along the wall and threw open a window. The gauze curtains blew inward and Maurice took fish-like bites out of the breeze. "It's the air conditioning you had installed, you see why we can't have it, he often reacts that way," Talitha explained with pride. Such a physical idiosyncracy, she believed, confirmed the originality of his mind.

Able to breathe freely again, Maurice was left with a soreness in his chest, more a result of his present irritation than the aftermath of past spasm. He did not care to be "explained" as if he were a household pet with difficult habits. "I am afraid I have never functioned well in any controlled environment," he said, resorting to his twinkle.

Cued in by the director's frantic gesture, Evans made up for lost time by jumping straight to the closing segment. "Your walls are literally papered with history," he said admiringly. "Do you think you are up to giving us a guided tour?"

Maurice sprang to his feet, moved across the room with a bouncy step that gave the lie to any previous display of infirmity. "Now here," he said, taking care to stand offside, "is a photograph you may find interesting—a group of us at the Kaiser Wilhelm Institute. What is the date there at the bottom? Ah, 1924. I had just arrived from Zurich, the new kid on the block, I believe you say, and there is one of the herr professors. Can you make him out? A Jewish name, difficult to remember—Einshtein? Yes, that was it."

Evans obediently laughed. Talitha too, because of the funny pronunciation. She followed on his heels, aware of another sound as soon as the laughter ceased, but took her cue from Evans, who was tensely ignoring it. They stopped before the case that once had so entranced her. The ribbons, medals, parchment scrolls—the detritus of fame, he would call it.

"We have here the detritus of fame," Maurice said. "Everything but the money, somehow that always gets mislaid."

Evans gave again his measured laugh, but Talitha's mind was elsewhere. Such a funny sound—animal, mineral or vegetable, she wondered? Perhaps the air conditioner, laboring now because of the open window. Then Maurice moved on and over his shoulder she saw the pigeon. It had picked its way along the broad inner sill to settle in the mulberry-patterned bowl Maurice had brought back from China. It had more the air of nesting for the season than roosting for the night, Talitha thought, biting back a smile, pretending not to notice. At any rate, she had identified the noise—that low throaty whirring sound like the gargle of blood in a deep wound. It was cooing.

~~

"Ah, Venus, I haven't had coffee like this since Vienna," Maurice crooned, savoring the faint odor of cinnamon. He was breakfasting alone in the kitchen, comfortable in his brocade robe with satin reveres, unwearable in Talitha's presence without invoking her laughter. She laughed the way the young laughed—cupping palm to mouth as if laughter were crumbs to be devoured greedily without spilling one. An endearing image as he recalled it but one that had forced him to contend with a Japanese kimono that stopped short at the knees and threatened him always with exposure.

"Well, I make it like Mrs. Stern taught me," Venus said, "she came from Vienna, I think, or some place like that. She certainly was fussy about her coffee. I'm a tea drinker myself."

"So," Maurice said, "my compliments to Mrs. Stern."

Venus turned her back. He was gratified to see that this reference to her previous employer met with so cool a response. Talitha is right, he thought: she likes us better.

"Where *is* Talitha?" hs asked with an explosive urgency that reflected his guilt in not having wondered before. His fingers played with the buttons of his robe's double-breasted closure.

The rigid back seemed to stiffen further. No, I was wrong, he thought with delight: she likes *me* better.

"She's out, that's all I know."

"Ah well, she's young, you see," Maurice said, much as he would have said, ah well, she's Chinese.

Venus addressed the stove. "In and out, in and out, all day long. And more out than in, if you want the truth of it."

Maurice's answer was to drink deep of his coffee. What man wanted the truth of it? Or was likely to get it. Or know it when he did. Truth as a monster from the deep—he drew pad and pencil from the pocket of his robe to jot down notes—the Gorgon's head, safely viewed only in a polished shield, mirror of the Self; for example, Hamlet, who looks on truth direct and is turned to stone . . .

"Hi there," Talitha said, so surprising him that he broke the pencil's point.

"Where have you been?" he asked before turning to see the answer in the large grocery bag cradled in her arms. To avoid the stare direct, he kept his querying gaze on the bag. It stared back from its imprinted blob of an unformed face, generic in its lack of detail: Have You Seen This Missing Child?

Talitha dropped her load on the counter—sufficient answer, she thought.

"You're spending entirely too much time in the sun," Maurice said in the defeated tone of a parent whose child will never listen. Her arms, he had noticed, were the same deep tan as the grocery bag.

"Just what am I supposed to do with these?" Venus asked, pulling out one, two, three clear plastic bags of tuberous vegetables, varying in size and shape but all with the same mottled dirt-encrusted look of freshly dug up roots.

"Oh Venus, I was counting on you to know how to cook them," Talitha said. She encircled Venus's broad waist to give a cajoling squeeze but the flesh of her arms drew back, distancing itself with a frisson of repulsion. As if under a microscope enlarging to monstrous proportions the smallest detail while narrowing the field, she examined the purplish-black mole on the mahogany-brown neck, the peculiar forward bend of earlobes like the cocking an animal's ears, the arthritic swelling of finger joints which the copper bracelet did nothing to diminish, a discolored flattened nail.

"I am not sure I am ready for such a chthonic cuisine," Maurice said.

Talitha did not look at him. "The truth is," she said—and was uncomfortably reminded that was how, as a child, she had always introduced a lie—"I have no idea why I bought all this stuff. Just to see what it tastes like, I suppose."

She took up a knife and whacked off the end of one of the tubers, revealing the waxy whiteness within. Cut a thin slice and made ready to take an exploratory bite. With a snort of disgust, Venus knocked it from her hand.

"What did you do that for?" Talitha asked in astonishment.

"You don't eat yucca raw, it'll make you sick," Venus said. "Better stick to your own kind of food."

Your own kind of people, Talitha knew she meant, and bridled. Venus spent entirely too much time in the laundry room, spinning gossip more than clothes. Talitha poured a cup of coffee and segregated herself with Maurice at the table.

"There was no paper delivery this morning," he said, gesturing to Venus for another pencil. "You must call them about it, they should adjust their bill."

"Oh, the paper," Talitha said, with a tsk of dismay. "I went out early just to get one and then forgot."

Common wisdom had it that a cup of coffee in the morning set the bowels moving, but Maurice knew better—it was the Times; without it, a costive grumpiness settled in for the day. Guilt impelled Talitha to explain that only her encounter with the Sospitian women could have driven so important an errand out of mind.

"I'm truly sorry—" she began but he had resumed his scribbling, did not look up. She tried again. "I wouldn't have forgotten except—"

"Forgotten what?" he asked with the mildness of inattention.

"Oh forget it," she snapped. An unnecessary injunction. Her annoyance abated as she realized she need not mention the Sospitians, for him an irritating subject at any time. The fates continued to be kind. Gratefully she reached for a croissant.

That the fates were operating, she had no doubt. Only the absence of the paper had driven her out of doors at that early hour when the Sospitian women did their shopping. Observing them close at hand, she felt a twinge of envy at the beauty which made of them a sisterhood. The flat planes of their faces that threw no shadows, presenting a smooth unlined surface whichever way they turned, reminded her of billboard art—a uniform perfection she had thought only an airbrush could achieve.

There were five of them, moving as a flock, cohesive in its progress but ragged at the edges, pecking here and there at one vegetable then another. Like a lost chick from another brood, Talitha trailed at their heels, stopping when they stopped, fingering what they fingered, buying what they bought, until by some subtle shifting of their order, she was in their midst. By the time they parted, Talitha had the comfortable feeling of being known by something more essential than her name, although with her goodby she shyly offered that. A solecism, she quickly realized, for they looked embarrassed and wheeled away. But not before one of them had brushed her hand, promising tomorrow. A mantra word, *tomorrow*. As was *tonight*. Tonight promised the drummers, whom she would watch and be watched by, from her own bench by the gate to the park.

She no longer had scruples about leaving Maurice alone. Only once had he awakened in her absence, to lecture her when she returned about the dangers of the night. Then that brief spasm of love-making, bite-marks left on his shoulder, evidence of consuming passion. Were they still visible, he kept asking, moved more by pride than concern. To extend his pleasure, she pretended to confusion as she had to passion. "I don't know what came over me," she would say.

What had come over her, she knew. He was old, old, old. The thought of his mouth on hers made her shudder—a dangerous intimacy with so deadly a disease. Better to nibble at palely freckled flesh and listen to the drumming still going strong.

She rose from the table, feeling light as a feather, as if relieved from the downward pull of a burden she had carried all her life. Passing around her husband, she leaned over to implant a kiss on his head, taking care to avoid the small liverish spot which blotched his tanned baldness. It seemed to her it was spreading.

"There she goes," Venus snorted, and would have said more except that she saw Maurice was working. (Oh I do like a man with brains, she boasted in the laundry room.) Holding her breath, trying not to make a sound, she wiped away the crumbs, removed Talitha's cup, a murderer intent on leaving behind no evidence.

~~

"You know you would have heard by now if anything had *really* happened," Venus said, as she had said so many times before. It was like giving a child its daily dose of tonic.

It was in that very circumlocution Maurice found such comfort, implying as it did that only violent crime and bloody accident were real—all else, including young lovers, existed solely in the imagination. It was a view the police took as well, he had noticed.

"Still, I think I'd better speak to Welkin," he said, but almost cheerfully.

"That's right," Venus said, "you get on to your lawyer. He'll tell you just the same, the longer you keep it out of the papers, the better for all concerned."

And Welkin said gently, "When exactly did she leave?"

Maurice was ashamed to admit he was not sure. There had been no dramatic slamming of the door. She had left in bits and pieces. Or had not left at all, he had just ceased to see her in bits and pieces. Venus would know—where was Venus? He forced himself to come up with some kind of date. "All I can tell you is she was going to a party and she never came back," he said and brought up his hand to serve as eye-shade.

To hide his tears, Welkin thought, moved to pity although—or perhaps because—this outcome was exactly what his wife had predicted on the wedding day.

Behind closed lids, drier than Welkin suspected, Maurice was concentrating on memory recall. All his efforts failed: the screen stayed blank, he could summon up no record of Talitha's face. He groaned—poor man, Welkin thought helplessly. Maurice wondered if he should share with his friend the grim certainty that somewhere in his brain a short-circuit had occurred, minuscule at the moment but signalling the onset of a progressive neurological disease, perhaps some rare form of visual agnosia such as had caused that man to mistake his wife for a hat. He decided to save it for his doctor.

Welkin sought for some comforting adage. The same old story. . . . there's no fool like an old fool . . . May and December . . . a vaguely remembered story from the Decameron. Not a comfort in the lot. He remembered the last time they had all been together, the picnic in the park, the cab ride home. Maurice had slammed the cab door shut, the driver pulled away, and his wife had started up. "If she hadn't brought it on herself, I'd feel sorry for that poor girl, did you notice how she looked at those men's legs?" He had told her to stop that cattiness. And now he would have to tell her she was right.

Swallowing his resentment, he leaned forward to evince concern. "Are you going to be all right?" he asked.

Maurice nodded. "Venus is taking good care of me," he said. This time the eyes were closed hardly longer than a blink. Venus. *Her* face appeared immediately, in all its wholesome splendor.

He bounced up from his seat to pace out his thoughts. A certain giddiness always came with a new idea. "I'm thinking," he said slowly, "Venus should move in. There's the extra bedroom down the hall, with its own bath, as private as she could want. It would be easier on her, that's the point. I worry about her getting safely home, she always stays so late these days. To make sure I'm tucked in for the night, she says." Maurice smiled to let Welkin know a good housekeeper must be humored.

Welkin noted there was something odd about his walk. The man looked frail. His wife had predicted that as well: "These old men who never seem to age—overnight it hits them and they fall apart." It was a change Welkin took umbrage at, as if Maurice had offered him a personal affront. Here was a man who had found a Shangri-La in the working of his great mind, who had grown foolish over a young girl and now was stranded, gasping for breath, in the low flatlands where he must die. It was all her fault.

"Not a bad idea," Welkin said.

"Not a *bad* idea?" Maurice stood over him, a combative stance. "I submit this is as good a one as I've ever had."

"A great idea," Welkin said. And perhaps it was, he thought, considering that the time soon would come when Maurice should not be left alone.

Maurice found even that too mild an approval. Venus was this, Venus was that, he so relished her name on his tongue he kept adding to the catalog of her virtues. "Just look at this—" he rummaged on his desk, threw Welkin a ledger—"doesn't she have a beautiful hand? Now I can tell where every penny goes. And she has a remarkable presence on the telephone—"

Welkin had enough of this dithyrambic ode. "A brilliant idea," he said conclusively. "And since you say she has no family to object, let's assume it's settled. As for the legal formalities, I'll take care of those."

"Formalities?" Maurice raised both brows. "Does one sign a contract for something like that?"

My God, he's already forgotten about his wife, Welkin thought. He took his leave without issuing a reminder, almost as cheerful as his client seemed to be. Laughing to himself, he rehearsed how he would greet his wife. A feint to the right: it's true they're breaking up. And then the knock-out blow: but Maurice is the one who has found another love.

~~

Never had sadness tasted so sweet as this fine day of autumn. Oddly, the sadness was not for his failing body— a "little" stroke, his doctor had called it, implying like a birthday wish many more to come—but for the blue wash of sky, the half-stripped trees, even for the weeds that had flourished summer-long in cellar doorways under iron gratings—like the art of children in concentration camps, he had thought—now rusty as the iron. It was as if not he but the world, this once-green thought embedded in his brain, were soon to die and on this morning walk with Venus he was paying his last respects. If so, he admitted now, it was the most beautiful thought he had ever had.

The forecast was for rain, hence this early outing, but as yet there was not a cloud in the sky. The benches along the park were already filled—the old seeking warmth, the homeless making a home.

"Too early for the park," Venus said, "we'll go where there are people." She was carrying her canvas sac, by which he knew two birds were being killed with one walk: give the child its daily airing while the marketing is done. They turned up the side street, crossing from the shaded side. Even those old brick buildings, now housing the Sospitians, held up their faces to the sun.

Venus held his arm as if making a uxorious claim. It amused him that they walked like lovers but that her arm was there to catch him if he fell and her steps, bustling by nature, were mincing to accommodate his shamble of a walk. His thoughts went back to the Alpine village where he was born. On that last visit, after so long an absence, he had hardly recognized his father. "You haven't changed a bit" he babbled to the dried husk that remained. Had to shout it again. "Nothing has changed," he shouted, including the village in the sweep of his arm. His father had looked up at him with something like a smile. "You're right," he said, "nothing has changed. Except—have you noticed how the ground now tilts and all the people speak in whispers?"

"Have you noticed," he asked Venus, "how the sidewalks tilt now?"

Venus thought he meant the cracks. "They're supposed to keep those fixed," she said. "If you fall you could sue them."

Venus would. Venus knew her rights, knew her worth. Knew the Lord and was willing to introduce him. In truth, he was touched to learn she prayed nightly, asking Jesus to keep him well. A non-invasive procedure, so why should he object? She took the added precaution of wiring him with copper. "I *know* it works for arthritis," she said. Arthritis was the least of his problems, still he wore the bracelet. She had woven it herself from twelve strands of copper wire—the number twelve, she let him understand having special application to good health.

Venus and her magic numbers. Mona Welkin making small talk out of transmigrating souls. ("My channel tells me—" that was Mona, coyly confessional—"in a previous life I was Anne of Cleves." He had pretended to forget which number wife that was. "Ah yes," he had made a play of finally remembering, "the one Henry called a Flanders mare.")

Even on recall, Mona's rage enlivened him, made him want to dance a jig. That maddened whinny: "I know you, Maurice, I saw you on TV. When it comes to immortality, you can place your trust in cancer cells, I'll take the human soul!" Ah Pythagoras, your wheel has turned, you are with us once again. The people have returned to eating beans, but who asks himself those three hard questions?

"Careful now," Venus warned him, "you're acting very spry."

"I'll wait outside," he said. He hated the supermarket. The ominous way the doors opened at his approach. The refrigerated air. Everything boxed or frozen or plastic-wrapped—desensualized. He perched on a hydrant as on a shooting stick, dreamed of the markets of his youth: the farmers' carts in the square, cabbages, leeks, artichokes, the tender lettuces (but wormy, wash them well), the vendors' formulaic cries, the old scales with their swaying pans, banks of flowers too, live chickens squawking, feathers flying when lifted by the feet, skinned carcasses slit down the middle, swinging from hooks—the colors, sights, sounds, smells—that was food!

Venus emerged, looking very smug. He gathered she had found some bargain.

"The manager saw you from inside," she said, "asked me if it was you—the one on TV. He'd heard you lived in the neighborhood, figured it was. A mind like that, he said—Venus mimicked the grocer's venerating tap on the head—is one in a million. He said he'd give anything to know what you were thinking so hard."

He felt a small lick of pleasure that his five—no, fifteen—minutes were not yet up. As for what he was thinking—he put on a look of lofty erudition. " A bad bargain," he said, "what I was thinking, he can have no understanding of."

"I told him as much," Venus said with satisfaction. He appreciated the gallantry with which she allowed him to take her arm. "Just one more stop," she said, "I need limes and they're cheaper at those little Spanish stores."

As soon as they turned the corner, he saw the women hovering around the outside bins. The sun abruptly lost its warmth, he felt the chill of winter in his bones. He had manufactured a false immunity to these Sospitians with his earplugs at night, choosing siesta-time for his walks. A biological mistake. He was defenseless now in their presence, devastated as by the virulence of a new disease.

"Every day there are more of them," he muttered, counting six. "They're taking over."

"There, there," Venus said, "you just ignore them. It won't take me but a minute, you can stay right here."

For all his fear and loathing, something about them drew him closer. Where did they keep their children, he suddenly wondered. He had yet to see their young. He enjoyed the conceit that these lubricious women, so redolent with sex, maintained their periods forever, never giving birth; that their men, for all their potent thighs, sired nothing.

He became aware that they were watching him as well—bird-like glances, always from the side. He lowered his gaze to concentrate on the play of hands hefting dark tubers, feeling strange fruit. In that air plaited with thin brown fingers, palely opalescent nails, one hand stood out, scarified at the fleshy tips, as if freshly healed from some injury. He followed that one to the cocked head and a sudden fury seized him, willing it to look at him straight on. It turned slowly, will resisting will. He almost crowed with triumph—he had won! Not that there was anything to see in such flat unreflective eyes. Jean Baptiste, Jean Baptiste, Jean Baptiste, the men had mocked him, telling him they were all the same. These women too, he felt sure, answered to one name.

A slight giddiness seized him, passed, still he was glad to see Venus emerge, elbow a path through the clump of women, send them scattering.

"Did you see how they blocked the aisle?" she grumbled, "you'd think they owned the place."

Her hate matched his, he saw—a bond more indissoluble than any marriage. Supported by the firm cushion of her arm, he looked at her fondly, taking in every lovely particularity. Venus was—Venus. No one like her.

"What are you looking at?" she asked, her short thick neck stretched to hauteur. She would always make pride her defense.

"You," he said—a word rich with happiness.

Her eyes grew larger, refracted by water. All the way home she held him to her fiercely, knowing how brief was the allotment of his days.

ABOUT THE AUTHOR

A native of Georgia, Rebecca Kavaler has been a recipient of two NEA fellowships and has published in Yale Review, Shenandoah, Carolina Quarterly, Nimrod and other journals. Her fiction has been selected for *Best American Short Stories* and the AWP Award Series for Short Fiction. Two collections of her stories and one novel has been published. She resides in New York City.